Undercover

BETH KEPHART

Undercover

LAURA GERINGER BOOKS

HarperTeen

An Imprint of HarperCollins*Publishers*

The Cyrano de Bergerac quotations beginning on page 28 are excerpted from *Cyrano de Bergerac* by Edmond Rostand, newly translated by Humbert Wolfe and illustrated by Simon Greco, Peter Pauper Press, Mount Vernon, NY, copyright 1941. Used with permission from Peter Pauper Press.

The excerpts on pages 81–83 from "Sonny's Blues" by James Baldwin come from *You've Got to Read This: Contemporary American Writers Introduce Stories that Held Them in Awe*, edited by Ron Hansen and Jim Shepard, © 1994.

Material on page 100 appeared, in a very different form, as "First Beginner" in *CALYX, A Journal of Art and Literature by Women*, Vol. 24, No. 1, Summer 2007 copyright © 2007 by Beth Kephart.

Material on pages 136–41 appeared, in a very different form,
as "The Drowning Girl" in *Peregrine*, Vol. 1, Spring 2005,
a publication of the Creative Writing Program of the University
of Pennsylvania. Copyright © 2005 by Beth Kephart.

The excerpt on page 167 from "Ars Poetica" by Archibald MacLeish comes from
www.poemhunter.com.

The excerpt on pages 187–189 is from "One Art" from *The Complete Poems 1927–1979* by Elizabeth Bishop. Copyright © 1979, 1983 by Alice Helen Methfessel. Reprinted by permission of Farrar, Straus and Giroux, LLC.

The poem on page 255, "Wild Geese" by Mary Oliver, comes from *Dream Work*, Atlantic Monthly Press, © 1986. Used with permission from Grove/Atlantic, Inc.

Library of Congress Cataloging-in-Publication Data
Kephart, Beth.
    Undercover / by Beth Kephart. — 1st ed.
        p.   cm.
    "Laura Geringer Books."
    Summary: High school sophomore Elisa is used to observing while going unnoticed except when classmates ask her to write love notes for them, but a teacher's recognition of her talent, a "client's" desire for her friendship, a love of ice-skating, and her parents' marital problems draw her out of herself.
    ISBN 978-0-06-123893-2 (trade bdg.)
    ISBN 978-0-06-123894-9 (lib. bdg.)
    [1. Love-letters—Fiction. 2. Poetry—Fiction. 3. Letters—Fiction.
4. High schools—Fiction. 5. Schools—Fiction. 6. Family problems—Fiction. 7. Ice skating—Fiction.] I. Title.
PZ7.K438Und 2007   2007002981
[Fic]—dc22   CIP
                                                                                        AC

Typography by Chad W. Beckerman
1 2 3 4 5 6 7 8 9 10
❖
First Edition

For my mother and father,
who gave me the gift of ice-skating.
And for my son, Jeremy,
the real writer.

—B.K.

paRt One

ONCE I SAW A VIXEN and a dog fox dancing. It was on the other side of the cul-de-sac, past the Gunns' place, through the trees, where the stream draws a wet line in spring. There was old snow on the ground that day, soft and slushy, and the trees were naked; I had my woolen mittens on. I was following the stream, and above and between the sound of the stream was the sound of birds, and also nested baby squirrels. The foxes, when I found them, were down by the catacombs, doing a slow-dance shuffle. Standing upright, I swear, palm to palm, with black socks on, red coats.

At school I didn't tell Margie about the fox dance, or David, or Karl. I didn't even tell Mr. Sheepals, in science, because it was what he'd call a non sequitur. My fox-dance story was an animal-kingdom story, and this was two years ago, second semester, eighth grade, when we were stuck on photosynthesis.

I have a sister, but she reads fashion magazines all day. My mother doesn't care for the woods. I kept my fox-dance story to myself, and I won't share it with others even now. It is my secret.

It's the other stuff I give away—the way I read the sky, the way I watch the sun, the forty-two flavors of breeze. It's everything people don't look for until it's too late, until they need a metaphor or simile to help promote their love. They don't have to come to me, but they almost always do. They know I've got it covered.

Dear Sandy, I'll write, pretending I'm Jon. *I came to the track meet to see you run, and it was like watching the lead bird in a migrating V. You were something else. Again.* Then I fold the paper and I slip in a feather from my Stash O' Nature box. The next day Jon will rewrite it all in his own way and sail the thing through the vents of Sandy's locker, and a week later, I'll see them—Sandy and Jon, so all-in-love together—going down the hall. He'll keep his eyes down, as conspirators do. "Hey," I'll say. "Hey," he'll mumble.

It's interesting to me, what others cannot see. For example: The precursors of leaves on trees, which can be seen only just in front of dusk, in March, when the setting sun turns the branches pink or some primary shade of green. Then there's the neon glow of the eyes on bees, and also the way a gerbera daisy starts out thinking it's yellow before it turns pink. Nature, you see, has a mind of her own. She's mysterious, and mystery is romantic.

Dear Lori, I write. *Last night I left my window open and a firefly flew through. So much light and all I could think of was you. Love Matt.*

2

M Y MOTHER AND MY SISTER could both be movie stars, and this is why: They are the same. They have corn-silk-color hair that dries slippery smooth and creamy, flawless skin. Their eyes are an interesting green. As people, they don't muss. My sister has had the same pair of white jeans for two months now, and they still look like new. My mother's pleated skirts are crisp, as if ironed with a ruler's edge.

My dad's so good at what he does that he's needed all over the world. In London, sometimes, and in Paris and Rome, or in Chicago, New York, and Boston. He'll take the morning's first plane, and a week or two later he'll come back home in the dark. We eat canned spaghetti on the nights Dad is gone. Mom talks on the phone with her green skin mask on, or studies her catalogs of seeds. Jilly lies stretched from head to toe on the family-room couch, taking note of skirt lengths and accessories.

My dad has put his lifetime of looking into a company that he calls Point of View. The logo is cool—an eye with a map drawn into it—and his business, he says, concerns perspective. Finding it, sharing it, applying it, leveraging it. *Leveraging*, by the way, is a word for the future.

I got my dad's curly auburn hair and altogether sensible-looking eyes. I got his pinprick freckles. And believe it or not, I got his double earlobe—one earlobe directly beside the other, like a lower case w—on the right side. It is for this reason that I do not wear my hair pulled back. Or bother with earrings. Honestly. I've got a couple of pairs of trousers and a couple of pairs of Keds and sweatshirts with hoods, for bad weather. Woolen mittens and turtle-necks for the snow-is-coming season. T-shirts and two white blouses for the sticky days of summer.

Dad likes to say, about both of us, that we're undercover operatives who see the world better than the world sees us, and this, I swear, has its benefits. For example: I can study Sammy Bolten's nose all through lunch, and he'll never, ever notice. Draw it in profile, if I want; write a caption under my drawing: Mount Pocono. Also I know just by looking when someone's wavering with love or dreary with longing or about to turn and flee. Point of fact: It takes nothing to see.

I FOUND THE POND by following the stream that lies in the woods past the Gunns' place. It was a day in early October, and the leaves of the trees were glorified with highlights of henna and gold. I'd gone to the woods to test out my theory that acorns in autumn have smells, and also to work on a little something for Karl, who had a big new thing for Sue. *You're the pink quartz in the sunlight, all sparkly and alive*, I conjured. *You're the feather that the bluebird leaves behind.* Those were good, but they weren't up to my standards. I still had some conjuring to do.

The squirrels were hysterical in the trees that day, hurtling off limbs like cannonballs. Above the squirrel circus was a big-winged hawk that rode a thermal, then flapped its wings to follow the stream. After a while I started following the hawk. I took off my shoes, and I went running through autumn air that was so acorn ripe that it crunched.

I didn't see the pond until I'd gone down a slight hill and turned left between more trees, until I had passed between blue spruce, oak, and maple and steered deep toward the old mansions that had vanished over time—fallen down, been bulldozed down, been lost but for their ghosts. Everything cleared, and there was this pond and around the pond was this garden that had grown up and been abandoned—some end-of-the-season hydrangea, some wood anemone, some weedy trees and other stuff that was, as my dad says, long past its prime. The pond was round and still and murky green, and beneath the surface things were swimming that I couldn't see, while above the pond, like a hole cut out of cloth, there were no trees, just sky and hawk. You could get out and over the pond by walking an old dock, and right near where the dock planking began was a shack, a sort of lean-to thing with a folded roof and lockless door.

For a while I just stood there staring at that pond. I parted some weedy trees to get a better look. I walked around to where the dock began and went out and sat and stared. That's when I saw the girl beneath the water's surface—the white sculpted girl that someone must have carried out and anchored in. She had a smile on her face, this marble girl, like she knew some things that I never would. She had a marble book upon her sunken marble lap; her hair was algaed green; her eyes were blank. More than anything else, she was so entirely, so admirably calm.

The point is: The pond had belonged to someone once. It had been dug out or built up, or something. It had been edged and gardened and statue blessed, and it had been furnished with its own splintery dock—old planks of wood that had been hammered together for standing on or fishing from. There was rubbish about, of the most interesting sort—Hershey bar wrappers, smashed glass, wound-up balls of plastic twine, an old and rusty fishing pole, a moldering paperback. You don't have to discover something first to be an undercover operative. You just have to know what to do with your find.

I sat on the dock and I studied the girl; I looked to the hole in the trees that was the sky and watched the floating, floating, floating of the hawk. I stretched out my arms and imagined the sovereignty of so much soaring. I thought of Dad in London, missing the best part of October. Track the changes and get back to me, he'd said before he left, and now here I was with all October in my reach— every color, smell, and sound. I wanted to take it all home and put it inside my box. I wanted to send it to Dad.

Here, for the record, is a list of things I've

managed to stow in my Stash O' Nature box: The little wave-tossed shells I've found along the shore when the sea was pushed way back, and also sea-glass chips, which make stained-glass light when you hold them to the sun. All variety of rocks, pebbles, and stones, including mica so fine that I have cut it with a knife—peeled it, like it was fruit or something. The shed skin of a local snake, though that has mostly turned to dust. The dried husk of a lotus flower that sounds like maracas when you shake it. Seeds and long seedpods. Pinecones and burrs. An empty nest that had been stormed out of a tree. Tree leaves, crisped. The very tip of a tail that a squirrel left behind. Bird feathers. Wishbones that I never cracked. The faces of flowers I picked in time to press between the pages of fat books. Beetle bodies and ladybugs that were all done with living. Three green cicada shells. A pile of acorns, each with its cap. Some Polaroids of passing clouds. A vacant robin's egg.

My Stash O' Nature box is not a shoe-size box.

It's the old hatbox I found in the attic. It's got designated spaces for each species of thing, and the empty nest sits right dab in the middle, crowned by the vacated egg. When I pull the box out from underneath my bed, I'm the utmost in careful. I never yank. I never shake, and in that way the goods stay safe. Nature is a force, but it is delicate, too. You have to take care of what you find.

Dear Sue, your smile is as bright as the bleached shells at the seashore. Lame. I can do better.

Dear Sue, I'm as empty as a cracked egg except when you're with me. No. No one would believe it.

Dear Sue, You are as perfect as the mathematics in a pinecone. Not my best, but better.

I felt sorry for Dad being busy in London, when all of October was right where I was and where a pond, at least for the day, had been left entirely to me. He said he'd gone and had a chat with Big Ben and had taken a meander through the Tower of London, but that was nothing, and he'd said so, when compared to what was happening with the sugar maple trees. He couldn't remember what order the colors came in, he said, and he wanted me to tell him. He couldn't remember if tulip tree leaves skipped right over yellow in favor of red.

Dear Dad, I'd write when I got home. *I wish you were here with me. The trees are staging the best-ever show. The orange is closer to pink in places, and the red can go straight off to purple, and some of the leaves stay the brightest of green so you can't forget how they started. This year you'd like the yellow leaves best. They're pure as gold. I don't think any of the birds are going south. They want to stay with the action.*

J ILLY IS NOT SOMEONE who would stop and watch the trees. She hangs with the Luscious Juniors crowd; you put them all together, and it's a clothes store. They know style like I know words. They walk, and there's a breeze. It was hard on Jilly when I moved up from middle school—she made it easier by pretending I didn't exist. I learn at lightning speed. Now the only time Jilly and I say hello in the hall is when there's no one there except for us, which, for the record, never happens. I'm the one thing and she's the other, and I do not cramp her style.

The girls in my grade keep their distance, too, and for me that doesn't matter. I don't mess with them, I don't score with gossip, I don't steal the lead in the school play, which, by the way, was *West Side Story* last school year. I'm not ever going to bump someone from a party list, because I'm on no one's roster. I don't even hang in the margins hoping for some kind of attention, and ever since Margie and I decided in eighth grade that we wouldn't be best friends anymore, I've kept my own best counsel. I'm the kind of girl you'd want for your boyfriend's science partner, and if once in a while my mug shows up as Student of the Month, that steals nobody's thunder.

I slipped Karl the best lines I had written for Sue when we were dumping trash from our trays in the cafeteria. The bell was ringing. I'd looked around before I approached him to make sure no one had seen, and he stuffed my lines directly into his pocket without even taking a look. "Thanks, Elisa," he mumbled.

"Yeah."

"Is this all I need?"

"You've got the starter kit, Karl. You're golden." With the second bell blaring, Karl went off. I slipped my hands into my empty pockets and went the other way.

A few days later I was at my locker collecting stuff for math when I noticed Theo Moses of Honors English standing beside me. He wasn't doing much, just standing there, hands in his pocket, sort of trying to get my attention but doing an awkward job of it.

"What's up?" I finally asked him, because it was weird with him just hovering there, not talking.

"Nothing much." Theo shrugged.

"Suit yourself," I said. "I've got math." And because math is a whole hallway in one direction and a turn and half a second hallway in another, I slammed my locker shut and started walking. "Numbers aren't my thing," I said to Theo, though

I shouldn't have felt, usually do not feel, the need for any explaining. "I get to class early."

"Wait up," Theo said, and despite himself he started to hurry, switching his backpack from his right shoulder to his left so he could cut the crowd more quickly. He'd hung a furry blue monkey on a key chain from his belt, and it was jiggling with his hustling. He'd gelled his short blond hair straight up in the front and had a gold dot earring in his supremely ordinary right lobe.

"Elisa," he said, and again I asked him, "What?" and this time he said, "I heard—Karl told me— about, you know, the notes and stuff."

"Have a girl problem, Theo?" I asked. Because I was precisely one turn and half a hallway from math now, and we were running out of time, and because sometimes, like Dad says, you have to move your clients along. Name the issue. Cut directly to the chase.

"It's not a *problem*," Theo said, the words coming out between his teeth in a snarly way that made him sound both embarrassed and threatening. How spikelike, I thought, is his hair?

"An opportunity then?" I asked, like I knew my father would.

"Maybe," he said.

"Who is she?"

"This is between you and me, right?" Theo said, as if we were best friends or blood relations, as if I knew a single thing about him beyond the fact that it was a big, wide stretch for him to be in Honors anything. Theo was an only child, I knew that. He played lacrosse, a bruisers' game. He had a bunch of guys who high-fived him, and girls who idly watched him. He was nothing special, Theo. Not until you looked at him.

"Sure," I said. "Sure." Just like that, because who cares?

"Lila," Theo whispered. "I'm in love with Lila."

"But—" I started, and then stopped. This is America, after all. Free market. Free will. Theo didn't have a chance with Lila, but was that supposed to

20

matter to me? I give out poems, not love advice. I do what I'm asked, no more. Lila's only going for seniors these days, I didn't say. Lila's only ever going to be with the captain of the basketball team.

"So you can help?" Theo pressed, for we had reached Mr. Marcoroon's door and there was an equation on the board I'd have to sit down and answer soon. He looked so—I don't know—vulnerable. He touched the dot on his ear, half smiled. Karl by this time had become Mr. Sue. Theo knew results when he saw them.

"Sure," I said. "Whatever, Theo. You can pick up the goods at my locker tomorrow, before the bell."

5

I HAD TO THINK. I had to go right back out to my pond and think. Because what is it about the world's Lilas that testosterone thinks it sees? Long, dark hair and tiny feet: I give her that. Eyelashes long, thin, and tangly as spider legs. A way of saying nothing that has everyone guessing what she thinks. A permanent, genetic smile inscribed upon her face.

She could never go undercover, the lovely Lila, and because of that she had my sympathy. Boys watched her constantly. Girls watched her, too— growing their hair out long in Lila style, dressing their feet in shoes a size too small, wetting their lashes with globs of Vaseline, as if that could ever add to their allure. She was defenseless against her own beauty. She could never show up anywhere and just be. Never be anything but a walking, high-gloss ad for the ultimate epitome of pretty.

"Lord above," I said to myself as I sat on the rickety dock at the pond, which was clearer that day, less agitated, more full of sky. The same hawk was up high and the air was acorn ripe and the marble girl was still reading her book, hadn't turned a single page in all this time. I wondered how it felt, to be sunk for all eternity.

Lila, Lila, Lila, I thought. And Theo, Theo, Theo. You'd have to be a calculus genius to make that equation work. Did he think his furry monkey was enough to catch her eye? Did he suppose she'd want to touch his spiky hair? Finger his gold ear dot? Whatever made Theo think he had a chance with her? Lacrosse was not basketball, never would be.

None of my existing metaphors would do. None

of the goods in my Stash O' Nature box. None of the poems in my head. Some subjects flat-out stump you, no matter how smart you are, and when that happens, Dad says, take a breather. I closed my eyes. I opened them. A leaf was falling from up high, and it was drifting down. It fell at last upon the pond and was drawn, by some secret force, toward the marble girl with the marble book upon her knees.

Track the changes, Dad had said, but the thing is: You can't count all the leaves. You can't name all the colors. You can feel the autumn coming, though, and in that turning there is mystery. *Lila.* I practiced Theo's note in my head. *Have you ever watched a leaf leave a tree? It falls upward first, and then it drifts toward the ground, just as I find myself drifting toward you.*

THREE WEEKS AFTER I gave Theo the
Lila note, I saw them walking down the hall
with their hands laced tight together. She was bending toward him, murmuring something, and he was
earnest beyond earnest, leaning just so close and listening. You'd think each stand-up-straight hair on
Theo's head was an antenna. You'd think his mouth
was a third eye, the way it was watching all her talking. Even his little blue monkey wasn't dancing so
hard. It was as if the two new lovebirds were all
wrapped up in a filmy bubble or stuck inside their
own Ziploc bag.

Whatever, I thought. Whatever. Because, like Dad says, we consultants don't do what we do for gratitude. We do it because it's an outlet for our talent, because solving problems is a form of exercise; we're just sharpening our skills for some future something of importance. Clients are the last people on earth who could ever be counted on for thanks. Dad says they always think, somehow, that if actually pressed, they could do the work themselves—fix the company, heal what's broken. Write the poem.

Fifth period was coming on, and fifth period was Honors English, Honors English being the one class I share with Theo. We'd been working on plays all semester long, and today's play was by a French guy—Edmond Rostand. I'd never heard of him, and I wasn't in the mood to care, and when Dr. Charmin began her context speech, I found my thoughts flitting up, around, and elsewhere—toward my dad, who had flown off to San Francisco that morning; toward the pond and the marble girl inside the pond; toward Theo, sitting three rows up and two people over, looking like half a person now, without his beloved Lila. I wasn't dialing into the lecture at all until I heard Dr. Charmin quoting from some critic: "'The great characteristic of Rostand's attitude towards the world he lives in consists of two things: a conviction of the necessity of what has recently been called "the lyric life," and a feeling that the average man fails to appreciate this necessity.'"

The average man fails to appreciate the lyric life. Well, I thought. What else is new?

By now Dr. Charmin was on a roll, going on in her sentimental fashion. "Rostand was a man," she was saying, "who dared, at the early age of twenty-nine, to write a five-act drama in verse. A man whose work is as important to our understanding of ourselves and of language as Shakespeare ever was." Dr. Charmin had a sob-up-in-her-throat way of speaking and blond hair that was much too blond for her pale skin. You had to fight your way through her love of language for the facts.

Still, she had gotten my attention, or rather this playwright Rostand had, and now I picked up the dog-eared, faded-to-gray play pamphlet that had been left on every one of our desks. *Cyrano de Bergerac* the play was called, and even as Dr. Charmin continued, I was flipping the pages, scooping up phrases, seeing what I could see for myself. "She's beautiful / as a peach amused with strawberries," I read. "So cool / that merely to see her is to enrheum the heart." Peaches amused with strawberries, I made a Note to Self. Enrheum, I thought. Be sure to look it up. And then there was this passage that would have caught anybody's eye, about the hero's fabulously gigantic nose—a Ninth World Wonder of some sort:

> 'Tis my delight to face the world thus snouted,
> for none but fools like you have ever doubted

that a great nose argues its owner lavish
gentle and brave, like me, and not a knavish
nincompoop such as you, whose featureless face,
which serves no purpose but its own disgrace
and some small entertainment for these fingers . . .

Who knew that the shape and size of noses was a subject contemplated and lyrically translated by very famous playwrights? Who knew, for that matter, that peaches had the capacity, despite their pitted hearts, to grow bedazzled and amused?

"We'll be reading *Cyrano de Bergerac* to one another," Dr. Charmin was saying. "We'll be thinking about chivalry and humility, self-sacrifice and love, identity and appearance, loyalty and yearning. We'll be asking these questions throughout: Tragedy? Or comedy? What is the emotional legacy of this play?" And then without further ado, as they say, Dr. Charmin doled out the parts—the multiple marquis, the officers, the sisters, the porter, a musketeer, a bore, Christian de Neuvillette, Ragueneau, Le Bret, Cyrano de Bergerac, and—to me, the ordinary girl in the back of the room—the object of all male desire, Roxane.

NOVEMBER'S DAYS are shorter than October's. The sun hangs that much lower in the sky, and the clouds, when there are clouds, are dense. Out by the pond only the steadfast birds remained—the black birds that I like to call ravens for effect but that are, in point of fact, mere backyard crows. "Where are you going?" my mother sometimes asked me. But mostly she did not. I opened the door, and I was gone.

Dad was, as he said, in a bad place with his work. Stuart Small, the San Francisco client, was a nuisance. No matter what Dad did, Small wanted more—wanted everything Dad knew and thought and then some. Every few days or so the guy would forget what he had originally commissioned, or change his mind, or fail to implement Dad's strategy, and then that would be Dad's fault—this failure to remember, this failure to act—and Dad would have to start all over again. "Working for pennies," Dad would say. "Working for peanuts and a long, tall glass of pain."

"You're supposed to be your own boss," Mom would say to Dad on the telephone at night. "And the front doorknob is broken and the back sliding screen door is off its track, and isn't that your job too? To be here with your family? To fix things? Whom do you love, Robert? What and whom? Make up your mind." And then my mom would stop and say she was sorry. Yes, she would say. Yes, she understood. Dad would say something to make her laugh, and she'd tell him that she loved him, and then he'd make her blush.

But the night before, the talk hadn't ended with

love, and when Mom hung up, she was crying. There were clear streaks down her powdery foundation. Her lips had lost their painted color and were two thin, pale-blue lines. Jilly was sprawled across the family-room couch, a nighttime soap opera turned on. "Mom," she said, offering up her ginger ale, "come here and watch," for this was Jilly's way, which was the way she'd learned from Mom: When bad things happen, grab a drink and an old worn blanket and lie yourself right down.

I went to the pond to think. I went to the pond, and no one found me, and when I came home nobody wondered where I'd been, or at least nobody asked. Most of the leaves of autumn were already on the ground, except for a few yellow flags here and there. There was a raven in most every tree, but not a single hawk to be found, and the sky was poked to bits with the nakedness of trees. The color of the day was the color of a storm that had chosen not to come.

You could think of the dock as one long rickety

stair that perched above the pond. You could think of sitting there all afternoon with your feet hinged down, watching the changeless girl in her autumn world, bright fallen leaves paddling over her head. I thought of all the things she must have seen and all she could not say. About the mansions that once had been and the people who had lived in them, all gone now. About how nobody but me had laid claim to the pond, at least not that particular autumn.

I thought about Dad. I thought about the hills he said he climbed every day and the famous people he saw in their everyday clothes and how trolleys supposedly went up and down with people hanging out their windows. I thought about the big granite wedge that was Stuart Small's building. Dad said the granite had a copper sparkle to it, and that no matter where you went inside the place, you felt like you'd been gleamed. Stuart Small was a little man who wore elevating shoes, Dad said. He'd shaved his head to give himself stature. He'd been buying other companies as a way of getting big, and now everything was cracking at the seams. Dad was there because Small needed advice, and that was Dad's forte—advising. Dad took thoughts that were messy and he made them neat. He drew out clear lines between choices. You could ask him what might happen and he'd paint a picture for you. You could tell him you were worried, and he'd listen.

Which is why I wished that Dad were back—because he'd know what to do with Lila's Theo, which was, by the way, what everyone now called him; he was that possessed. He was Lila's Theo, and he was at her side morning, noon, and probably night—between classes and in the lunchroom and, whenever weather permitted, on the sloping turf of the school's front yard, a place we all called Romance Hill. Romance Hill is where new lovers go to announce their loverhood. It's like taking out an ad on *The New York Times*'s front page.

Except, in the quiet before school actually began, before Lila's bus had turned up in the line, I had

Theo to myself, or he had me. All I ever had to do was show up at my locker, and there he'd be, sort of prowling around, wanting to talk but not wanting to talk, wanting my advice and also wishing he didn't need it.

"Elisa," he'd say.

"What?" I'd answer.

"You have something?"

And because he couldn't say it, I tried to make him. Sometimes that's the only power you have. "Something like a poem, you mean?"

"Something like that."

"Something for Lila?"

"Come on, Elisa."

"Yeah, sure." I'd shrug, handing him the latest rendition of love on a balled-up piece of paper. I'd watch his face as he read.

And that was our ritual. That was our thing. The poems themselves were like little nothing poems— two-line metaphors with no real beat, no lasting magic, just something Theo could slip into the girl's locker before her bus dropped her at school. The poems made Lila sweet for Theo. They made her turn her liquid eyes on him, walk beside him on her tiny feet, wrap her hand up tight in his.

You are the moon and the stars that surround the moon and the galaxy beyond the galaxy we live in.

You are the day when it's returning to itself, the start of every color in each dawn.

Your name is the name that doves will sing when calling to each other, tree to tree.

I knew the work was lame, but Lila didn't, and that's what mattered, at least to Theo, who would take the words and rewrite them as his own and slink off down the hall, his little blue monkey dancing. I'd tell myself it was nothing, pretend it was as easy as it had always been, but the truth was I was growing weary. Language is not a bottomless well, and also—it gets tedious, being on love's lookout for others.

Besides that, Theo was a client like no other, needing something jazzy and new every day. My other clients had only ever needed a line or two, and then they would take it from there. But Lila, I was learning, was insatiable—had Theo dangling from some kind of love-poem string. She needed adoration. She needed it in words. She needed it daily. The situation was headed for trouble. And now when David asked for help, I had to tell him I was booked. When Lyle needed attitude, I said, "Go watch some movies." I didn't know how to cut the cord with Theo. I'd started feeling sorry for him, and how I hated that, and also: Theo was kind of cute. Yes, you had to look at him up close to notice, but then you really did.

I kicked my feet out over the dock and watched the shadows. I looked up at the birds in the trees and wished I could fly. I saw that the sun was setting, but I was too tired to move, and I'd come up empty of metaphors. Dad would have known what to do, I was sure. Or at least he would have listened, if I'd cared to talk it through. But it was San Francisco where he was and November where I sat, and I was growing chilled to the bone.

IN DR. CHARMIN'S class I still could not guess if Rostand's play was tragic or funny. I mean, it is funny—isn't it?—that Cyrano, the one with the monstrous nose, composes ballads during swordfights and odes in pastry shops. And it's funny too how dimwitted Roxane's lover Christian is, as if God had spent so much time fashioning the guy's precious looks that He never got around to his brain.

But playing Roxane made me feel uncomfortable. For there is Cyrano, writing letters to Roxane on behalf of the local pretty boy, and there is

Roxane, buying every bit of it, hook, line, and sinker. Why can't she see that it is Cyrano's heart and head inside those letters? Why can't she tell how much he loves her? And what does this say about people in general, that they can't see what is standing before them? Beauty rules, every single time. Beauty is the password.

We had reached Act IV, the battle scene in which Roxane appears at the battlefront overflowing with her passion for Christian, going on about the letters she so loves, letters he didn't write. "Read it with emotion, Elisa," Dr. Charmin instructed, and at first I really did do my best while Jimmy Dowell, aka Lurch, stumbled through the words written for Christian.

Lurch would read:

> *Now tell me why you came*
> *by roads whose thousand terrors*
>   *mock the name,*
> *facing the brutal soldiery and the*
>   *Ritters*
> *to join me?*

And I would say:

Dearest, you must blame your letters.

To which Lurch would say (loud and insistent, the way Lurch always says it):

What!

To which I was to answer:

If I risk danger, all the fault is theirs;
they sweetly drugged me with divine
*   despairs.*
Think how you wrote, how many, how they
*   grew*
from beauty into beauty.

And I did say that, I got myself through "beauty into beauty," but beauty is a hard enough word to own when you look the way I do, a hard enough word to deliver in such a way that your classmates to the front of you and your classmates to the left of you will hear it and be persuaded.

"Again, Elisa," Dr. Charmin interrupted. "You're mumbling."

Lord, I thought. And sucking in enough air to blow a grandparent's birthday candles out, I repeated. And now Lurch, bizarrely eager, read on, his voice so loud it was as if he were performing through a megaphone. As if he were daring me to answer him with equally enthusing declarations:

> *For a few*
> *brief letters of love!*

The first moment I let pass might have been read as a dramatic pause. The second moment was strange. The third roused Dr. Charmin to high impatience. "Plays are like conversations, Elisa. Conversations are about listening and responding. Every time you pause or mumble, you take us outside the story; you interfere with its meaning." I felt the eyes of some of my classmates turning my way. I didn't want to make a scene. I just wanted to be excused from one. I clamped my mouth hard around the words, loudly enough, but without any apparent feeling:

Be still! You cannot guess
how I have loved, with what bright tenderness,
since underneath my window a voice unknown
revealed your spirit to its true stature grown.
For all this bitter month (my love, rejoice!)
far in your letters, but sweet, I heard that voice,
which since that evening clothes you like a cloak.
I heard. I came.—

"Excuse me," I said. "I'm sorry." Cutting it off right there, unable to read the next line, unwilling to contribute any further to the farce. Tragic? Funny? What is the word for a rhyming five-act play that little by little leaves you feeling so exposed, so cataclysmically stupid? So ashamed.

"Elisa? asked Dr. Charmin.

"There's something in my throat," I said. "I can't."

"But you are Roxane, Elisa."

"I'm sorry, Dr. Charmin." I coughed. I felt my face flare, a red-hot, stoked-up fire. Whoever hadn't already turned to stare at me just did, so that I was suddenly, awfully visible. No undercover operative now. I stared at my shoes and then I raised my eyes to three rows up and two seats over, where Theo was looking back at me with a look I might have almost called concerned, or sympathetic. His eyes seemed bluer than I'd remembered, his hair not so spiky.

"Margie," Dr. Charmin called, hands on her hips, her mouth tight. "Will you please assume our heroine's part? Elisa, go get a drink of water, will you? And then come back to class."

I pushed out to stand up, and the little nubs on the chair legs made their protesting squeal. I left the class and went down the hall toward the silver water fountain. I drank and drank until my eyes got wet. And then my eyes were so wet I couldn't see.

THAT AFTERNOON I went straight to the pond. I threw my backpack through the porch door and I went off through the cul-de-sac, past the Gunns', and into the woods, between the mass of old burned-out rhododenrons and the naked oaks and tulip trees, down to the stream that was, this time of year, just creeping along, all congested with old leaves. The sun was already falling out of the sky, and my parka wasn't thick enough for the wind that was blowing so hard that sometimes the ravens in the trees seemed tossed off their limbs. Snow, I thought, because the clouds were overwrought, because whenever I exhaled I saw my white breath.

When I finally reached the pond, I saw that changes were afoot. That the water had started becoming crystalline and the marble girl was freezing in. All around her and above her was the stuff of early ice, and suddenly all I wanted was to relieve her of her trap. She wouldn't be able to breathe, I feared. She wouldn't be able to disappear, either.

I try, as hard as I can, to be my dad's best girl—reliable and solid. I try to take each thing as it comes and to forsake the sentimental. But that afternoon the cold and the wind and the poor girl's condition made my eyes swell up with tears. Made my throat hurt again until I had to yell, and my yell was a boom, it was a thunderclap, it was what I didn't know I had inside me. I was the only one around, save for the ravens. They took to the skies in a black swirl.

Dear Elisa,

Things have gotten worse with Stuart Small. He shouldn't have bought Sole Food without an integration plan, and the management teams don't get along. Small says he's looking to me to play referee, but he's not interested in listening. He's like those squirrels you see out in the middle of the street that go this way and that way even as the big trucks keep coming.

You can't walk out on your clients though. So it looks like I'm in this one for the long haul, Elisa. I miss you and I miss Mom and I miss Jilly. I'd need a few of your best metaphors to be able to say just how much.

> *Love,*
> *Dad*

10

BEFORE JILLY became the world's most accomplished couch potato, she used to go ice-skating with my mom. Just the two of them, down at the Border Road Rink on Saturday afternoons at five. I always thought it was mostly about the fashions—Mom with her little fur-collared coats and Jilly with her white, puffy muffler. I couldn't really picture them doing the stroking or twirling you see on TV—couldn't imagine either one of them losing, even for one moment, her breath. And falling down? Forget about it. They had too much loveliness for that.

We'd have pizza on those skating nights, and if Dad was home, he'd light us all a fire. A big, roaring, marshmallow-roasting fire, though only Dad and I ever ate the marshmallows; Mom called them sugar pills. I liked those nights, sitting by the fire next to Dad, our two sticks side by side in the flame, but those nights are long gone. Now Mom's and Jilly's skates hung by a nail on our basement wall, beside a lot of other junk no one remembers, but whenever skating is on, that's what they watch, with me watching too. Measuring all those complicated moves, cheering whenever big stuff gets done—the double axels and triple lutzes, the laybacks and camel spins, the triple-toe-loop combinations that it'd take years of sacrifice and some kind of genius to learn.

One day after the early freeze had settled in, and floating things had become static, I dared to walk across the entire pond, and the ice hissed and snapped but held. One day I ran halfway across it, then slid to the opposite bank. One day

I sat on the dock and stared out over the gleam, and that was when I remembered my mother's skates and all that I'd seen on TV. The next day I carried those skates with me, under my jacket, so no one could see. I sat at the edge of the dock and laced them on. They fit me like a glove.

When a pond freezes over, it's not just ice and gleam. It's frozen twigs and old gum wrappers, insect wings and gray fish tails and any number of things you could take for bug eyes or buttons or coins. It's like the whole history of the pond pushed up and stuck hard on itself, except for the marble girl, who stayed where she was, anchored to the bottom. I could hardly see her, but I knew she was there, and when I started skating, when I first pushed out onto that ice in my mother's skates, I skated for her, because, no matter how bad you are, no matter how awkward, freakishly earlobed, ungraced, you need an audience.

It was like walking at first, walking badly with my arms out at my sides and my knees sputtering forward, and if I didn't avoid the biggest frozen-in twigs or the bronze spots that looked like bug eyes, I'd bump up like I was letting loose with some gigantic hiccup, and one foot would go east and the other would go south, and I'd be down on my knees, but soon I was up again, and soon after that I was gliding. Not pushing straight back now, but pushing out side to side, and in this way I learned about edges and speed.

Sometimes I'd look up and I'd see the ravens watching. Sometimes I'd take my parka off and *S* one arm into an arabesque, the way a pretty girl might do. Sometimes I'd clap my hands to make an echo, and when I did that the ravens all took to the skies, turned themselves into acrobats, faked like they were falling and caught themselves before they crashed. Or they started dueling in midair with a twig, or playing raven catch with some odd brown thing, and then, afterward, they'd settle back into the trees and hunch their shoulders and crank their heads and look at me with their accusing eyes.

"I'm skating now," I'd call to them, and they'd call back: *Kirrk, kirrk, kirrk, nuh nuh; caw caw caw; nuk nuk*. Which is poetry in raven speak. Which is another metaphor.

Lila, your voice is the song of birds when they've been touched by moonlight.

Lila, the clouds are promising snow. Soon the world will be as lovely as you.

Lila, I'd slide across the planet for you, and then go sliding around again.

Lila, you are so much lovelier than poems. Let's forget about words for a while.

But Lila wouldn't let me forget about words. Not even for a moment. Lila wouldn't let me forget that I was too much like Cyrano. "See! how the poor heart can mock its own emptiness," said Cyrano. Said I.

I T SNOWED, and it snowed. I could hear the crystal flakes knocking around inside the whistle of the wind. Downstairs Jilly was warming herself by the glow of the TV and Mom was on the phone nearby. She'd gone five steps up in the stairwell so that she could speak in so-called private, forgetting—it was just so like her—that I was lying on my bed, eight straight-up steps above her, my bedroom door flung wide enough to hear.

"Old dresser lifts up with the wind and flies out of the pickup truck ahead, and before there's anything to do it's through Carrie's windshield. That's the way I heard it. At least that's what Walter said," my mother was telling Mrs. Garland from across the street. "Or maybe it was a spare tire. A big one off the back of some diesel." Mrs. Garland is my mother's best neighborhood friend. She sleeps in her pearls and makes fruited Jell-O and is so proud of her arms that she goes sleeveless in winter, and besides all that, she holds the *Guinness Book of Records* record for gossip.

"Anyway," my mother continued, "dresser or spare. It doesn't make much of a difference. Nobody should ever live through that."

"*Should* is what I said," my mother insisted after a pause. "I said nobody *should*."

"Of course I'm going to the funeral," she said after some silence. "Everybody's going. Aren't you?"

I was trying to write my Cyrano paper. I started humming to myself like bad TV actors sometimes do. Hmmmm. Hmmnh. MMM. Hmmmm. Hmmnh. MMM. Turning my own noise into brain silence. I had come down squarely on the side of tragedy, because there's nothing remotely funny about unrequited love, nothing even possibly ha-ha about talent such as Cyrano's going to the sole and exclusive use of promoting someone else's love affair. Cyrano is a tragedy made more tragic by the humor, was my thesis. And now—hmmmm. Hmmnh. MMM. Hmmmm. Hmmnh. MMM—I was trying to turn my argument to art. I was trying not to think of Theo and Lila. I was trying to remember the too many rules and wherefores of citations.

When I came up for brain air, my mom was still nibbling away with Mrs. Garland.

"I miss him," I heard her saying. "And then I get angry about missing him. And then I feel like the worst wife on the planet. But why should Robert assume that I'm just going to lie around here and wait? It's that assumption that I mind most of all. His client *needs* him, he says. *Needs* him? But isn't he needed at home?"

Outside, the snow was coming down harder, as if

there were bits of stone inside each flake. All the way across the country was San Francisco, wrapped, I imagined, in a deep and baffling fog. I rolled off my bed and peeled my curtains back, and it was clear, even in the dark, that the whole east coast was going under. The flood lamps in the neighbor's yard were heavy with ice. The old brown ornamental grass along the hedge was cracked and scary. The deck had an unnatural look to it, and the branches of the trees had a diamond's glare; limb after brittle limb seemed sure to snap. I could feel the cold on the opposite side of the glass.

THERE WAS NO SCHOOL the next day, and I was out of the house by dawn, hours before Mom or Jilly would ever dream of getting up. The yard was not a yard anymore; it was a crystal quilt of white. The Japanese maple looked like it had been taken over by a flock of white birds, and the bench beside it looked as if it had lifted up and floated. There were no people out, not even the evidence of people, and I remembered how my dad once said that if you dug deep enough in our neighborhood, you'd find the archaeology of hundred-year-old parties and abandoned pleasure gardens and the footings of the old stone houses that had not survived. You can listen for the sound of ghosts, Dad once said, on a summer night when it was just the two of us. But in snow that deep and that new you don't hear anything but yourself—your boots in the snow, the thoughts in your head.

I wanted to tell my dad what Mom had said. I wanted to put it in a letter. But what I'd heard I wasn't supposed to have heard. What I knew wasn't mine. That's the thing about being undercover: You know what you know, and you cannot act on it.

The way to the woods had disappeared beneath the snow. The evergreens on one side of the street were bent like half a tunnel. The snow came up to my knees and fell back inside my boots, but the coldest part of me was my lungs, which felt all scorched and steaming. By the time I crossed the cul-de-sac and went past the Gunns', I was in another country. I was the first female explorer of Antarctica. I was the one survivor of the Holocaust. I was alone like nothing and no one had ever in the history of the world been alone, and then I saw the fox.

He was on the other side of the snowed-in stream. He had a yellowish chest and the prettiest auburn hair and a smart pair of ears, and also, this is the truth, he had a raven. The bird was oily and so black that it might have been purple, and when it moved one wing, just slowly opened it and closed it, I understood that it still had the twitch of life. That if I ran after the fox, it might release the bird, and if the bird were released, it might fly. But I also understood that it wasn't my place to interfere, that it wasn't my place to choose between them.

I leaned against a tree.

I tried to breathe.

Dad, I would write in my letter. *You need to come home. Please. Get back to me.*

What happens to bees when it snows? I wondered. What happens to dragonflies? How do monarchs always know their way back home, across a million miles? These were the questions I'd ask Mr. Sheepals if I weren't an Honors sophomore now, and already supposed to know.

Dear Elisa,

San Francisco has hills that fall off into the ocean and a bridge that burns red in the sun. Down by the wharf they sell miniature shrimp in Dixie cups, and that's where I am right now—at the wharf, writing to you.

It isn't your fault that the raven died. Think of all the living that it did before that, the privilege it was given to fly. When I was a boy, that was all I wanted—to grow a pair of wings and get up into the sky. I had a basement full of failed wing projects. Boards and capes and motors, even a pile of found feathers I once tried to glue together with a bottle of Elmer's; you should have seen your grandmother's face. But I never got any higher than the backyard fence I'd launch from. I never got inside a cloud. Your raven did.

Love,
Dad

D R. CHARMIN HAD SAID that I was to report to her after school, and I was, shall we say, disinclined. Going mano a mano with most teachers is not my idea of a good time, and in imagining myself with Dr. Charmin after school, I got no comic relief whatsoever. Once she asked Shelley Fisch to copy out an entire chapter of a book she had not read. Once she made Missy Sweeney sit for two whole hours in absolute silence to teach her a little lesson about in-class gossip. Dr. Charmin was my high school's only Ph.D. She thought the whole place stood in her shadow.

It was a week after the big snowfall, and it was cold. I had my backpack strapped on and my mittens pulled tight to the wrists, and I was chewing the soft inner pink of my lips, because I didn't know why I was there. "Elisa," Dr. Charmin said, "sit down," and I did, leaning forward in a front-row seat without taking one ounce of gear off.

"I wanted to talk with you about your paper, Elisa," Dr. Charmin said.

"I'm sorry, Dr. Charmin," I said, because if there's one thing Dad's been very clear about, it's that the client—or the teacher—must always be kowtowed to.

"Sorry for what?" she asked.

"For whatever I didn't do right, I guess." Now my inside lip was really sore.

"You're not in trouble," Dr. Charmin said. "I just wanted to talk with you."

I could feel my face turning the color of shame and also relief, which are possibly two separate colors, an ugly clash. I wasn't in trouble, but there I sat, waiting for whatever would come next.

"'Cyrano is a tragedy made more tragic by the humor,'" Dr. Charmin said, quoting from my paper. "An interesting proposition, that."

"I thought so," I said. I mean: What else?

"Is something going on with you, Elisa?" Dr. Charmin asked.

"No," I said. Too quickly. "No. Why do you ask?"

"'Cyrano can't hide his monstrous nose, so he hides behind his humor,'" Dr. Charmin read to me, from me. "'He hides behind his words, and that's like death. No one can ever see Cyrano for who he is, least of all Cyrano himself. No one can ever prove to him that he's worthy of Roxane. Love isn't fair, it just isn't. And beauty is the worst kind of lie.'" Dr. Charmin's skin was paler than usual. She had a spiderweb of a pin stuck in above her heart and worry lines across her face. "Elisa," she continued, "that sounds serious."

"Serious assignment," I said. "Serious response." My backpack was heavy and sweaty on my back. I peeled off my mittens. First my right one. Then my left. I looked everywhere but at Dr. Charmin. I even closed my eyes. "I should have copyedited," I said after she said nothing. "I'm sorry."

"It's good work, Elisa. That's not the point. The day you couldn't read Roxane? What was it?"

"My throat," I said. "My throat got dry."

"There's no one in this room right now but you and me, Elisa," Dr. Charmin said warningly.

"I know," I said, and really I did, and I was using every trick in every book not to cry. I was thinking about the pond and the girl in the pond. I was thinking about the seals of San Francisco. I was thinking about how it would be if Dad came home for Christmas, and how it would be if he didn't. I was wondering if Dr. Charmin lived alone, if her house reeked with the smell of old books. Panache, I thought to myself. Panache. But still my eyes were burning.

"If you want to talk to me, Elisa, you can," Dr. Charmin said, between tightening lips.

"I'm fine," I said. "I really am."

"I gave you an A on your paper." Dr. Charmin leaned forward on her desk and stared hard and into me. She straightened and stood and faced the chalkboard, then turned back around with her lecturing face. I stood, for it seemed it was time to go. I fixed the backpack on my back.

"Appreciate it, Dr. Charmin," I mumbled.

"You're free to go," she said. I noticed how thin the skin on her face had gotten. And how much paler, too.

"Thank you, Dr. Charmin," I said, and my backpack was like a ton of bricks and I was hot as Hades. I ran down the hall, though hall running isn't legal. I ran every single block back home through the wintry world.

Lila,

 *Last night the moon was as big as
an orchestra playing a song for you.*
      Love, Theo

Lila,

You are the card I was needing to be dealt.

Love, Theo

Lila,

It was a red fox in the snow, and I wanted the color of its coat same as I want you.

Love, Theo

Lila,

    You know how a river goes on and on? That is my love for you.

                 Love, Theo

14

"IT'S UP TO YOU," I was telling Theo, "to decide." It was Tuesday, and most of the snow had gone to wherever snow goes—underneath the grass, I guess. Down the sewer lines. Beneath the iced-over stream.

He was standing near my locker; this was his early-morning habit now. My habit too—I had begun to get there early, begun, in spite of myself, to look for him, to imagine, against my better judgment, that we were pals or something. That we had more than a Cyrano conspiracy. His hair was longer now than it had been, and the spikes had grown soft and fell forward; he'd replaced the gold-colored dot in his ear with a tiny silver circle. When he talked to me, he looked at me. When I laughed, he laughed along too. The night before, I'd gone overboard with the Lila poems, and maybe it's true that I was hoping that in them he'd see the genius of me, the beauty of my words in his hands.

"Well, doesn't it depend on her mood," he was asking, "if a card is right, or a moon?" He was sifting through my masterpieces, one by one. I stood against my locker, proud.

"She's your girlfriend, Theo." I said it like I felt sorry for him, like I could convince him to feel sorry for himself.

"I guess."

"I wasn't trying to confuse you."

"Right." He looked up and he smiled, that great Theo Moses smile.

"Options, Theo. It's all about options. Just give her the one that fits." I grabbed my math book and my notes from science lab. I raised my eyebrow, laughed. A couple of the buses had just let out along the curb near Romance Hill. "Don't look now," I told Theo, "but she's coming."

"Lila?"

"Your moon. Your card. Your—"

"Yeah," he said. "I get it," and maybe he'd have said more except that Sammy Bolten was slithering by. Sammy, who has always been hot for Lila, and for whom I won't write a single word. He asked me once, end of eighth grade, and I said no flat out. There are those who don't deserve the blessing of our talent. Sammy Bolten is one of those.

"Trading down?" Sammy said to Theo, giving the once-all-over to me. You could have won Olympic gold if you'd ski-jumped down his nose. You could have tobogganed straight to China. What could it matter, what he thought of me? He was the biggest whatever on the planet.

"Leave it alone, Bolten," Theo said. "Shut your trap." He wasn't slumped against the locker now; he'd stepped sideways, stood much straighter. I looked at Bolten. Looked back at Theo. How can it be that a fight begins precisely where something pleasant was?

"Shut my *trap*?" Sammy said. "Did I *hear* you right?" He jabbed his elbow into Theo's rib cage. Theo didn't flinch.

"Go to Hell." Theo's voice was even and hard, and suddenly Sammy was pitching forward, his face red.

"You know the way there?"

"Follow your nose," Theo said. "It'll get you there pretty quick."

Sammy pressed closer, raised his fist: "You know where this will take you?" Theo took two steps forward, and now they were standing nose to crooked nose. I was standing there too, and I couldn't decide if Theo was protecting himself or saving me.

"Just let it be, Theo," I said. "He doesn't matter." But already we'd collected ourselves a rubbernecking crowd. One more bit of threatening fist and we'd have Principal Kiley writing us up for promoting an unauthorized spectator sport on school grounds. There was Margie, who'd already passed on by, making her way back down the hall. Sue and Mr. Sue were hovering. Even Jilly was there—I could see her sea-green eyes looking bigger for all their underlining. And now here was Lila, in her little sculpted coat, with her black hair swooshed up into one of those messy knots you just know she spends two hours on. Great, I thought. Like we need Lila.

"Theo?" Lila said in that whiny, dumb-girl voice of hers that puts a question mark at the end of every sentence.

"Hey, Lila." Theo looked past Sammy to Lila, then to me.

"What're you doing?" Lila had tucked a loose piece of hair behind one perfect ear, and you could smell her—lavender or lilac or something. With the super-high heels that must have killed her to wear, she came up eye to eye with Theo, or almost.

"Nothing, Lila," Theo said. "Doing nothing." He gave Sammy Bolten a little shove back toward the crowd and fingered the silver in his ear. Sammy made a move like he was going to push back, but we were saved by the bell.

"With *her*, Theo," Lila persisted, looking up at me, because even with her sizable heels I had her beat. "What're you doing with *her*?" I got my second once-all-over in as many minutes. I looked at Theo, and I looked at his hand, and at the papers that I'd folded into squares. Hide them, you idiot, I wanted to say. Put them in your pocket. Now.

"You don't actually *like* her, do you, Theo?" Lila said, coming even closer and wedging in next to Theo. She hooked her arm into Theo's sweatshirt. She gave him a big-eyed look.

"*Like* her?" Theo said. Looking from me to her, from her to me, looking at Sammy Bolten, who still hadn't the sense to walk away. Theo turned a shade of red you find only in my mother's garden, and I stood where I was, and I waited. Go ahead, I thought. Answer Lila's question. Do you like me, Theo? But nothing.

You're the keeper of your own dignity, Dad always says. You're the one who shapes your own story. I didn't have many options, and I wasn't about to be defeated. "English, Lila," I finally said. "Fifth period. I was asking Theo for the assignment." Theo stared at me and then he looked away. Lila kissed his lips in triumph.

I saw Margie slinking back down the hall. Saw Jilly falling in with the High Fashion crowd. "You're a nerd," Sammy Bolten said. "Nerds don't forget their assignments."

15

WHEN A DAY STARTS like that one had, all you can hope for is that it'll come speedily to an end. That one didn't. It dragged on through math, it dragged on through science, it dragged on through Spanish, where I could not conjugate one single verb. In the cafeteria they were serving macaroni and cheese. I forced it down with two cartons of milk. I didn't go anywhere near Theo and Lila, not even close. Stayed away from Jilly. Watched Sue and Mr. Sue, who had both brought sandwiches from home. They were trading halves, as lovers do, splitting the Cheez Doodles.

But it was hard not to get a burn off of Margie's glad glare, which attached itself to my every swallow. Hard not to remember another humiliation, two summers ago, when Margie and I went like always, just the two of us, to see the Fourth of July fireworks show, in the football field behind the high school, where there were already so many people and blankets, sparklers and little miniature flags, and those light-up tubes in neon colors that people wear around their necks at night. The town shoots the fireworks off the tennis courts each year. They keep two fire trucks standing by. When the fireworks go off, you try to give each one a name— that's a tadpole; that's a rocket; that's a dandelion loose in the wind. No one sits through fireworks alone. It just isn't done, where I'm from.

Except that night when I was smoothing Margie's purple blanket across the thirty-yard line in the field, and Margie went off to the concession stand to get us Cokes and never did come back. She was gone a long time before I understood, gone even longer before I believed it. The sun was falling down, and then it was gone, and then people started fizzing up their sparklers, and then someone starting singing the national anthem over the P.A., and still Margie wasn't back; I was alone. And then the first rocket wheeled high and split the sky in two, and then it banged big and there were all those bits of fire floating. Then that one rocket was followed by all the others, by the screaming, streaming bangs of light, until the sky was burn and color and the air smelled like pop guns, and it was almost like being at war all of a sudden because Margie had gone off to get us Cokes and she wasn't coming back, she'd found another crowd to hang with, kids so much cooler than me. She'd found her chance and taken it that night. I wouldn't answer the phone when she called after that. I wouldn't listen to her apology. I still have her purple blanket, balled up in the corner of my closet.

By the time fifth period rolled around, I'd gone forty days and forty nights in misery. All I wanted was to be alone and especially—especially—I did not want to be in class with Theo. It's one thing to be invisible, and it's another to be dismissed. Theo was crazy if he thought he was ever getting another Lila poem off me. I walked the long way to my chair, through the blaring of the bell, and I slumped down to painfully unload my things.

"This is Honors English," Dr. Charmin was saying. "I expect you to read like adults. Think like adults. Thinking adults read 'Sonny's Blues' slow. They listen for the sound of the words, not just their meaning.

"The opening lines, please, Margie," Dr. Charmin continued, and Margie, in her squeaky-trombone voice, began reading James Baldwin's words: "'I read about it in the paper, in the subway, on my way to work. I read it, and I couldn't believe it, and I read it again. Then perhaps I just stared at it, at the newsprint spelling out his name, spelling out the story. I stared at it in the swinging lights of the subway car, and in the faces and bodies of the people, and in my own face, trapped in the darkness which roared outside.'"

"What is the author doing here?" Dr. Charmin prodded. "What is he doing? Margie?" I looked at Margie with her reddish hair and freckles and thought about how once these things had bonded us like sisters. Something can go to nothing in no time flat.

Margie was snapping a huge wad of gum and taking her time with the question. "Saying the same thing over and over?" she finally offered.

"Talking about a character reading the paper on a subway?" Jonah perked up. And he was being serious.

"Staring like this?" Sarah Waxner said, doing a cross-eyed stare until half the room cracked up. As if any of this were funny. Suddenly I was feeling sorry for Dr. Charmin, who was trying her best.

"Turning the sentences into a song." There was no other choice. Again. So I said it.

"Okay," Dr. Charmin said, tipping a smile at me, glaring at Margie and Jonah and Sarah and all the others who had not raised their hands. "That's a start. At least one of you is listening. Now concentrate, please, on the passage I'll now read. Close your eyes and listen. This is coming much later in the story, just a few paragraphs from the end. We already know about the troubles Sonny's had. We already know how he's suffered, and yet—the tragedy he writes of is inseparable from its beauty.

"'All I know about music is that not many people ever really hear it. And even then, on the rare occasions when something opens within, and the music enters, what we mainly hear, or hear corroborated, are personal, private, vanishing evocations. But the man who creates the music is hearing something else, is dealing with the roar rising from the void and imposing order on it as it hits the air.'"

Something caught in Dr. Charmin's throat, and she stopped. She looked up, and in the corner of one eye there was the wet smudge of a tear.

"A poem about anything that moves you. Anything that roars."

"How long does it have to be?" Theo asked, and I nearly killed him with my eyes. I burned a hole into the back of his ridiculous head. I cut his furry monkey loose and made it dance.

"The right length," Dr. Charmin answered.

"Well, how long is that?" Sarah asked, turning back toward the class again and rolling her actress-big eyes.

"Long enough to tell a story. Short enough to persuade me it's true."

"Very helpful," someone sniggered. And almost everyone in Honors English groaned, then started collecting all their goods. I myself didn't move an inch. I was waiting for Theo to scat.

16

AFTER SCHOOL I was three of my eight blocks from home when I heard Theo calling my name. "Hey," he said, "wait up." A couple of times, he called me; but I wouldn't turn. Theo lives in the other direction from me, where they're turning cornfields into houses. All you would find if you were digging where he lives is seeds, or maybe an old Indian arrowhead, which makes my part of town, and also everything about me, vastly superior and never ever once again a thing to be dismissed.

I didn't stop walking, but he was running. There was the smell of snow in the air.

"Could you just wait up?" he called. "Elisa?"

You know how in movies the girl is always running from the guy, and the guy catches up, and then it's romance? Well, that was not what this was about. "What're you doing here?" I called behind me. "Your house is that way." I pointed.

"Come on, Elisa," Theo said, and from the corner of one eye I saw him slipping on slicked snow, catching his balance, and still running. His face had turned a chap-burned red. His jacket was unzipped, his monkey dancing.

"What do you want, Theo?" I was walking faster and faster, and I still had speed in me. Every time I breathed in, I burned my lungs with the winter air. Every time I breathed out, I made a cloud. The faster I walked, the faster he ran. He kept on shortening the distance.

"I don't want anything, Elisa. Just hold up."

"Wouldn't be you if you didn't want something," I said.

"Give me a break, Elisa. Give me a minute."

He was a half a step behind me now. He reached his hand up to my right shoulder and pinned it there. "Aren't you afraid someone will see us, Theo?" I asked. "Mistake us for friends or something?"

"Shut up, Elisa."

"'You don't actually like her, do you, Theo?'" I did my best imitation of dumb-as-a-doorknob Lila. "'*Like* her?'" Now I was imitating Theo. "'How disgusting,'" I exaggerated. "'How thoroughly, totally fur ball. No, I don't like her. No, I couldn't like *her*. She is smaller than a squiggly thing in a microscope to me.'"

"I wanted to explain about that."

"That's nice, Theo. Really. Is there something to explain?" Theo had turned me around so that we were facing each other. He'd put his second hand on my second shoulder. I stared straight past him.

"That I do like you, Elisa. You're my friend. I made a mistake back there."

"I'm your *Cyrano*, Theo. Not your friend."

"Maybe it started out like that. Maybe—"

"Give it up, Theo. What do you want? More stuff for Lila? Help with Dr. Charmin's poem? A new thesaurus for your birthday?"

"Why are you being such an idiot, Elisa?"

"Me?" I said. "That's a good one." I wrested my shoulders free of his grip. I turned and started running, and after a while, after a block or two, I stopped and looked back, but Theo had disappeared.

One moment changes everything. One moment, and everything you almost had is instantly, mournfully gone.

17

I COULD NEVER TELL YOU all the names of every TV skater I ever envied, but I can tell you about this one I won't forget. She was gorgeous and dark and a little strong, and it didn't matter whether she was gliding or leaping or spinning or bending, it was the music that carried her from the rink's one side to the other, the music that made her beautiful. Imagine music gushing down the hollow places in your bones, and making you liquid, and giving you speed. Imagine music turning your body into a song. That's how it must have been for her. That's how she made it seem.

In the woods that night the old snow had turned to slush and the muck of animal tracks, and there were sapphire shadows between the trees. The sound was my boots in the snow, maybe the hoot of a winter owl. The sound was the thin trickle beneath the stream that had mostly frozen over. I was running fast as a fox, running and running and not for one second caring if I fell, or if I tripped, or if my hair was wicked wild, and sometimes there was the snap of twigs from way up high, or right beneath my feet, but all I cared about was the frozen pond and the pair of stolen skates I'd left in that old abandoned shack. All I wanted was to glide from the pond's one end to its other, over the head of the immovable marble girl, with one foot down and the other one stretched out and high behind me, my arms like wings. I would bend my knees and I would jump right up to the big and starry, inexhaustible sky. I'm not talking fancy stuff—no way. Not axels, not pick jumps, not fancy spins. I'm just talking about what a girl might do by her lonesome, on a pond, in the dark.

Here are some of the names, for the record, of the moves I've so far mastered: crossovers (which is just a way of rounding bends), Mohawk (which is a way of turning backward), spread eagle (which is pointing your one foot east and your other west and leaning back into a curve), spiral (which is holding one leg high behind you), waltz jump (which is the littlest nothing hop of a jump, but still a version of fantastic when you're me), lunge (which is dragging one foot behind on the ice), the basic posture of an Ina Bauer (which is easier, I am finding, than a spread eagle), and your very basic blurring spin. Here is how I skate: with music spilling directly through my bones. When I'm on the ice, I'm where the story begins. I take an Ina Bauer on the diagonal and arch back so that I'm dialoguing with the moon. I bend my knees at the launching of the waltz jump and hold that leaping-forward part until gravity hauls me down. I ride the middle of my blade when I ride a spiral, and when I spin, I pull the whole world in tight, until I'm all wrapped up in love. I don't care how I look, you see. I just care how I feel.

It is a fabulous thing, skating at night. I can think of a song, and the song will turn itself on, and it is the only thing that matters for a while. I can lift up my arms and my soul drifts. I can bend and my knees will be percussion. I can twizzle and my hips will be a mash of the divine. Maybe I'm beautiful when I'm skating at night. Maybe I'm the queen of the stars.

That night I rode a Bauer down the center of the pond. I put a spiral on an edge, then lunged. I did a waltz jump and another waltz jump, until I had gravity in my pocket. I skated for what felt like hours, then sat for a while on the dock. Out in the woods I could hear the crunching of sticks beneath the feet of squirrels, the hooting of an owl, the wind. If there were deer between the trees, they hid in the shadows. If there were raccoons, they were one hundred percent stealth. I didn't know where the ravens had gone. I imagined them clumped up in trees.

The moon and the stars and the distance went by. I thought about Dad in the hills of San

Francisco, about Mom in the house, about Dr. Charmin alone in her house with a hundred million smelly books, about Margie and her new friends, about the girl in the pond and the mystery I still had not decoded. I thought about Theo and about Lila, about invisibility and dismissal, about running away and maybe, although I didn't know it myself, hoping to be caught. And then the tears came back and I couldn't think anymore. Making and roaring, Dr. Charmin had said. Write about something that's true. Skating is true. Skating and the music in the hollow of my bones.

In the woods the crackle of breaking twigs and crunched-over snow was becoming a more noticeable sound. A whole gang of squirrels, it seemed to me, maybe a deer, maybe a sleepwalking, smudge-faced raccoon, but when I looked out toward the woods, the only thing that I could see was lots of trees and shadows. Nothing, and yet how should I explain the sound that was coming toward me, moving forward? Then, finally, I saw it.

It was like two incredibly tiny stars fallen straight

down from the sky. Just the smallest fractures, little reflections of light that twinkled on and off, like Christmas lights. They were lights, but they weren't lights. They were stars, but they couldn't have been, and suddenly I understood that what was coming closer and closer was a pair of eyes. The eyes of a dog fox headed for the pond, but where was the vixen? I scanned the woods. I held my breath. I waited.

Have you ever had a fox call out your name in the middle of the woods at night? Have you ever been talked to by an animal? Because that night this is what happened to me: a fox called out my name. "Elisa," it called in a voice that seemed familiar. "Hey, Elisa."

I sat there on the edge of the dock, paralyzed.

I sat there, and the dog fox kept walking.

"Theo?" I said after a minute. "Theo?"

"Hey," he said. "Lord, it's cold." And kept on walking in my direction, like it was no big deal, like he had not just somehow undergone a fox-to-person metamorphosis, like I hadn't run from him for hours, like I hadn't been dismissed. He had black gloves on and a black cap. He was acting as if he belonged.

"What are you doing here?" I demanded. He had rounded the pond by now and was coming up the dock, and I was facing him, still sitting down with my mother's skates on, my mouth gaping open, my hair gone wild.

"Does a guy need an invitation?" Theo said after he'd finally made it to where I was sitting. He plunked down. He rubbed his gloves together and blew some air at them. He pulled his cap lower on his head. I knotted my arms across my chest. "I followed you here," he said. "I've been watching a long time. Cold out here."

I stared straight across the pond. I slithered over to the left so that our shoulders wouldn't be touching. I'd thought he was stars and then I'd thought he was a fox. I had thought I'd been alone, but I hadn't.

"I had to come because you wouldn't listen."

"Wouldn't listen?"

"This afternoon, Elisa. Remember?"

"Lila know you're here?" I asked after a minute.

"I don't tell her everything."

"Well that's a real tall glass of comfort," I said.

"Do you have to be so hard, Elisa?"

"Hard like the ice, Theo, or hard like complicated?"

"You'd qualify for both," he said, and maybe it was the way he said it, or maybe it was that he'd come, or maybe I was sick of being stuck so hard with my own hard self, but all of the sudden I wasn't angry anymore. I turned my head and took a good look at Theo in the moonlight, at the silver circle in his ear, at the black cap that made him seem just that much older. How do you know when an apology is true—when it means something, or can change something, or will last outside the moment? Hold the moment is what the skating pros on TV say. Keep yourself over your blades. I couldn't remember being this close to a boy ever before.

"You've been watching me skate all this time?" I started the conversation again, after a while.

"Sort of. Yeah."

"My mother's skates," I said, dangling my feet

out in front of me. "I stole them."

He didn't say anything at first, and then he laughed. "You're one of a kind, Elisa Cantor."

"The one and only," I said, and then there was nothing more to say, so we sat together staring out at the woods, at the blue between the trees.

"So what do you want?" I finally broke the silence. "For real?"

"I want you to believe me."

"Believe what?"

"That I'm sorry for this morning. Shouldn't have happened. Bolten's a schmuck. And Lila—she just gets jealous."

"That's a good one, Theo. Lila jealous of me." I laughed when I said it, snorted the words straight through my nose.

"You have something they don't have," he said, after saying nothing at first.

"Like really bad hair?" I heard myself say, and again I started to laugh, and this time Theo started laughing too, so I raised both hands and pushed him. "I'm the only one who can laugh at that," I warned him, and I jumped down off the dock and started off across the pond, over frozen-in twigs, fish eyes, wings. I skated all the way to the opposite end, and Theo kept getting smaller, until finally he was on his feet as well—running across the pond in his big black boots, tripping like a fool, falling down, sliding. He looked like some comic-strip monster trying to dance on tiny toes. He looked nothing like a fox with his fair skin. I could have skated circles around him, and soon that's how it was—me cutting in front of him and throwing a hop of a waltz jump, me taking off and jumping whenever he got close. Finally he just sat down in the middle of the pond, all curled over, breathless.

"You need a pair of skates, Theo," I told him, and he said, "I suppose I do."

And I said: "You better not tell a soul."

"About what?"

"About my pond."

Vixen 🍂

This part is true:
I wore my fat gray parka and my hair was wild
and I skated alone,
first ordinary and square above the blades,
then more plastic in the knees
and my arms out
and my hands
and a little bit of something in my hips.

You know how a song is time,
and how you turn and you turn on the blades
* of time,*
and you close your eyes
and maybe you leap
and you are the girl with the wild hair
and the big parka
on the hard and complicated ice.

That night:

It was much too cold for most people
and the stars seemed upside down
and someone on the Weather Channel had said
that a blizzard was on its way.

18

A T SCHOOL MOST PEOPLE kept their distance more than usual. Sammy Bolten was making like I didn't exist, like I had never blown right by him. Mr. and Mrs. Sue were Mr. and Mrs. Sue, oblivious, and Margie talked to the new friends she had behind a freckled hand—little puffs of heehaws and giggles. Whenever I saw Theo and Lila together, I mostly saw Lila, wrapped tight as a vine or maybe a snake around Theo—showing who was whose, curling the loose parts of her hair around a finger, kissing the soft part of Theo's unpierced ear, acting like she'd never worry a day in her life about losing any microcell of her latest locked-down possession.

Still there were the mornings, before Lila's bus rolled in. Still Theo passed me at my locker, sometimes stopping if there was no one else about, sometimes telling me some dumb joke he'd heard, or some new old news about lacrosse, and when he did that, when he was just mine and nobody watching, I felt something hopeful crack inside me, something almost miserably sweet that made me want more than a girl like me ever has the right to want. I wanted to be strong, my own person, not Theo's Cyrano. But most of all I wanted Theo, or the sort of proximity to Theo that friendship brings. I hated myself for ghosting those poems. And I knew I'd hate me even more if I weren't Theo's confidante.

And then one morning, when I was handing Theo a new batch of my very best metaphors, Lila came earlier than she was supposed to come, striding down the hall with a big trifold poster for health class. Someone had dropped her and her awkward cargo off, obviously, and it flapped and slapped her as she walked the hall; its cardboard wings stretched out, snapped back, caught wind. She wasn't the least bit happy to see her Theo at my locker with a bunch of something in his hands. She telegraphed her condemnation from fifty lockers down. She was all dark stare and steam rising.

"Give them back," I said to Theo, who seemed frozen all of a sudden.

"What?"

"The poems. Give them back to me, Theo. I swear." It was as if he had forgotten what he was holding in his hands—proof of his duplicity, and of mine—and if a mean little corner of my heart maybe wanted to be found out, maybe wanted Lila to be forced to choose between Theo as he actually was and Theo as she thought him to be, I also knew that being found out would force a choice for Theo. We were undercover friends, Theo and I. Our cover was Honors English. If Lila knew about the metaphors, it would destroy our covert standing.

"What's she doing here?" Theo said. "I mean, this early?"

I would have grabbed the metaphor stash from his hands myself, I would have slapped him into action, but now too much time had passed. Now any rushed or guilty-looking thing that happened between Theo and me would be seen for what it was and prosecuted. There was only one thing to do, and that was to make like the moment was run-of-the-mill. Make like the little words in Theo's hands were part of protocol.

"Hey, Lila," I said, because going on the offensive is always better, Dad says, than being forced to defend.

"I swear to God, Theo," Lila said, ignoring my greeting entirely.

"Skeletal system?" I said, taking a quick glimpse at her poster.

She wouldn't look at me. She stared at Theo.

"I did my health poster on vision and perception," I said. "But that was back in ninth grade."

"Will you shut her up?" Lila said, not lifting her dark, violet-shaded eyes from Theo for half a second.

"Hey," I said. "We're done here. Don't worry."

"You're done what?" Lila said, still not looking at me.

"Same old same old," I said. "Honors English."

"Metaphors," Theo said, snapping back to life at last. "We had to grade each other's homework."

"Yeah? Well? This poster's heavy," Lila said, thrusting her trifolded bones Theo's way. "You saw me coming, Theo. You should have helped."

"My bad," he said.

"Here, Theo," I said, nodding toward the metaphors, "give me those." As if I were trying to take a load off his hands so that he could help the princess with her towering bones. He pushed the love bits back at me, held the trifold like a shield. Lila saw someone she knew and waved. Theo threw a quick smile my way.

"See you," I said.

"Around," he said.

· · ·

The thing about *Cyrano* is that Christian dies just after he and Roxane marry and long before the two ever do know each other. Christian never has to confess. Roxane can hold fast to her preposterous fantasy. Cyrano's the only one who knows the truth, and Cyrano says nothing. He allows— *encourages*, even—the memory of the handsome poet. He leaves Roxane with her falsely footed memories.

All through school that day I was thinking about this—about Cyrano not telling what he knew. I was thinking how puny the human rib cage is when it has to hold something as huge as that within. When you're undercover, you have to keep things to yourself. You have to go around with a who-cares? slouch even when there are fists of anger, fists of wanting, all inside you, pounding. I had a right answer for Mr. Marcoroon and made like it was easy. I wrote a letter to a fictitious pen pal in Spanish, revealing nothing. I read a book at lunch and never once looked up at Margie. I gave Theo the thumbs-up in English when he thumbed-up at me. And when Dr. Charmin asked to see me after school that day, I simply said okay.

So that's where I was—in her classroom after school that day, with my undercover operative posture on. When Dr. Charmin asked if I could wait one moment, I started counting the books on her piled-up desk, the number of pieces of chalk in the box, the variety of pens and rubber bands and markers. The stacks of sticky notes. I started counting, and it was a way to stop feeling the fists that kept pounding, pounding me.

"Thank you," Dr. Charmin finally interrupted herself, "for coming to see me." She looked up at me and sort of smiled. She looked as if she could use some sun; the woman was positively ghostly.

"Sure." I shrugged.

"It's about your poem." She stood now, maybe so that I could see her better, or maybe so that she could see me. She wasn't very tall, that Dr. Charmin. But she had presence.

I looked at my feet, at my beat-up, snow-stained canvas shoes, at the ugly speckles in the linoleum floor, at nothing. I looked at the floor, and I wondered what she saw when she looked at me.

"'Vixen' is lovely," she said at last. I looked up to see if she was telling the truth and saw the thousand crisscross lines on her forehead. Her eyes were the color of a storm, and honest. She had a jeweled Christmas tree on her lapel.

"Oh," I said. "Thank you." I breathed in, and I breathed out.

"You have talent," Dr. Charmin continued. "Do you know that?" Which is a very funny question to be asked, and not like funny ha-ha, but like odd. My dad says you have to master two things in life: modesty and confidence. You can't answer a question like that and score in both categories. I went for saying nothing.

"What are you going to do with it?"

I shrugged my shoulders, glanced again at the floor. "I don't know."

"What are you doing with it now?"

I shrugged again. "Nothing much." I was feeling like maybe Dr. Charmin was onto me and my stupid ghosted love notes. Maybe she'd interrogated Theo or something, or maybe she just knew. Maybe you can look at an invisible person and see that she's not there.

"You're in tenth grade, Elisa. It's time to start thinking about your future."

I waited for her to say more, but she didn't. I waited for that shock of being known. But if she wasn't going to mention my love notes, I certainly wasn't going to either. "Okay."

"I'd like to help you do that."

I didn't shrug this time. I couldn't. It had never occurred to me—never once—that she could be an ally.

"So let's begin with this," she was saying. "What are a writer's two best friends?"

Writers don't have friends, I almost said. That's how they get to be writers. But instead I guessed the obvious. "The imagination?"

"Yes." She nodded. "And words." The criss-cross of lines on her face smoothed to stillness. There was actually a little color in her face. And now she removed a book from the top of one pile and walked around to my side of her desk. "This," she told me, "is my own Book of Words. I started it when I was about your age, and I'm still adding to it."

She placed what she'd been holding in my hand. It was a dull-gray journal with a ton of what seemed to be coffee mug stains on the front and a dark-blue spine that was ungluing at one end. Inside it had words and definitions written in a thousand different colors. Sometimes the words were in cursive, sometimes they were not. Every once in a while there was some one long thing set out in quotation marks, or a bunch of arrows chasing each other in a circle. None of the entries were alphabetical. You'd have had to remember where you'd put them in the first place ever to find them all over again.

"Cool," I said.

"I have so many favorite words," she went on, but not really to me. I slipped off my backpack, sat down in Margie's chair, and opened up the journal. I flipped the pages backward and forward, forward and back, then finally stopped at one:

> **Minion**—best to use when expressing contempt
>
> *Feckless*: See Mark Lawson
>
> ERSTWHILE is former, but ERSATZ is inferior.
>
> N e g a t I v e C a p a b I l I t y = see John Keats, October 27, 1818
>
> **Temerity** is more abrasive than **audacity**.

"When," I asked Dr. Charmin, looking up at last, "did you write this page?" It hardly resembled her chalkboard writing. There were cross-outs and smudge marks. It was messy.

She came toward me and I gave her the book. She flipped back a few pages and squinted. "That was 1974," she said, after she'd decoded something. "Freshman year of college."

"Oh," I said. I couldn't picture that. I couldn't picture her in jeans or anything. I couldn't picture her being younger than she was. I needed work, it was clear, on my imagination. "What did you do with the words?" I asked her.

"I learned them," she said. "I made them part of me. I used them to help me understand the world—and then I used them to name things. That's what writers do. And that's what you are— a writer."

"So the words belong to you?" I asked her, thinking about my pond, thinking about the marble girl in the bottom of the pond, reading the book that had no words.

"No. The words belong to anyone. To anyone who cares. And I think you care, Elisa."

I felt my whole face go hot, the skin turn red beneath my freckles, my hair doing a triple somersault away from my head. I could hear the minute hand of the classroom clock tocking off the time and the sound of a basketball being warmed up in the gym across the hall. Dr. Charmin herself was frighteningly quiet, just standing there with her arms folded across her chest, waiting for something. Waiting for me to say the right next thing, I guess, but how could I know what that was?

"I like to write metaphors," I finally confessed. "And similes. I like to take what I find and make it an equation. Like colors are flavors. Or seasons are stories. Or clouds are ideas. I like to see what I see and turn it into words, but I think it's getting harder. Or maybe I peaked. Or maybe there's nothing new to be said. I don't know." I shrugged.

"What do you mean?" Dr. Charmin untied her arms and leaned against her desk. She smiled, and now something new was happening with the lines in her forehead. I had never talked to a teacher like this.

"Like in the 'Vixen' poem I couldn't think of what I could put in the hips, so I guess I sort of cheated," I finally confessed. "'A little bit of something in my hips.' Sorry," I added. "That was lame. I guess."

"So you need more words," Dr. Charmin said.

"Maybe."

"That's what I thought." She turned and started picking through the stacks and clutter on her desk, placing her own journal in one corner. I drummed my fingers on the bottom of Margie's chair, wondering what was next. I had that can't-swallow feeling on the top of my tongue, a knot that wasn't hunger in my stomach. "Never any time like the present," she said at last, turning back toward me, "to begin." I took what she was handing to me. I opened it up and quickly flipped through. It was a book made up of all blank pages. Just page after page of white blankness.

"There's nothing in here," I said.

"Well, that's the point, isn't it? You have to find

your own words that fit. And when you do, this is where you'll keep them."

"Is this homework then?" I asked, though I should have just said thank you.

"No. It's a challenge. See how far you can take things."

"Okay." The clock on the wall said 3:35. The game had begun across the hall; I could hear the whistle of the referee, the cheering of the parents in the stands. The sky outside was hanging low, full of cold and weather. I stood. I gathered up my things and hung my backpack on my back. I held the wordless book in my right hand.

"Find the words you need," Dr. Charmin said. "Write more of your own poems."

"My own poems," I echoed.

She looked at me with those big storm eyes.

She said, "You know what I'm talking about."

AN EPITAPH is what they write on tombstones. An epigraph is the thing they stick at the front of books. Something that announces the story's purpose or starting place. Something that puts readers in the mood.

That's what I wanted for my Book of Words—something to return to whenever I lost my way. Dad would have called it Strutting Out the Old Henry Ford, because that guy was good for about a billion sayings and because Dad started most of his projects that way, with Big Words from a Big Person to get the client in the mood. Ralph Waldo

Emerson was also huge in the sayings department, and so was Winston Churchill, and there were plenty of others, too, in the books Dad had on his shelves. So I started there, behind Dad's office door on the second door, with his best books of sayings all around me.

Language most shows a man: Speak, that I may see thee. That was Ben Jonson, and that was plain dreary.

The only interesting answers are those that destroy the questions. A Susan Sontag quote, and I had zero idea what it might mean.

A poem begins with a lump in the throat. That one courtesy of Robert Frost. I found it sentimental.

Jilly was on the phone down the hall, talking to Elaine about their latest shopping spree. Mom had Mrs. Garland over for Christmas decorating. They'd dragged a small, sweet blue spruce into the house and boxes of lights in from the garage, and out of the basement they had pulled the crates of ornaments and crèche scenes, mistletoe and tinsel.

Their talk smoked up the stairs and under Dad's office door, and even though I concentrated on the sayings, I heard every word.

"Men never tend to their own gardens," Mrs. Garland was saying in her authoritative voice. "They take advantage and then they take for granted. Oh, and doesn't that look nice, with the white lights."

"Gorgeous," my mother said. Then: "What I find unnatural is the presumption that they give us a ring and their father's last name and then a house and some children, and that's romance. But romance is noticing what we do to stay new. It's being here and feeling lucky that we don't belong to someone else. Doesn't he miss me?" my mother wanted to know. "Doesn't he want me to miss him?" She was pulling at something, grunting. She was scraping a stool across the floor.

"Everywhere I go, men are losing their minds," Mrs. Garland said. "It's epidemic."

"Not *all* men," my mother sniffed. "Angie's Tony

is a peach, don't you think? And what wouldn't you give for the way Mike looks at Maude?" There was the sound of a hammer pounding a nail. There was a scratch, and then: "The blue one, don't you think? With the red bow?"

"You have to give Robert an ultimatum, Tina," Mrs. Garland said. "What else can you do?"

"You mean: Come home now or I'm leaving? You mean: Hope you like the hills of San Francisco, because you can stay right where you are and never bother coming home?"

I knew my mother was showing off for Mrs. Garland. I was sure she couldn't mean what she was saying. Almost sure. But did you ever feel like your soul has morphed into a volcano with all the rocks and everything else about to spew? Ever get so your throat's so clogged up tight you can't breathe unless you cough? Because that's what happened to me: I started coughing. Lying on the floor in Dad's office, beside the million quotables, looking for an epigraph, listening to Mom, I started coughing, and it was the kind of coughing that happens when you cannot breathe, when you smack the floor to stay alive, smack your chest, smack the air itself for air. I coughed so hard you could have measured it on the Richter scale. You would have thought the world was splitting in two.

"Jilly?" I could hear my mother between the spasms. "Honey? You okay?" I could tell that she'd moved to the bottom of the stairs, that she was working her way toward deciphering the commotion, to weighing things out in her head.

"NOT JILLY!" I spat out. I was sprawled out flat on my back by now, wheezing like a smoker.

"Elisa?" my mother asked a minute later. I didn't answer her. I made her suffer. I tested her. She didn't come. "Elisa?" she called again. "Please. Answer me."

I coughed, but it wasn't much, it wasn't frightening. It was an I-don't-need-you and I'm-not-answering-you cough, is what it was.

"Elisa!" my mother said.

"Just let her be," said Mrs. Garland after a while. "There's nothing for it." I could hear them stepping away from the stairwell now, returning to their business. I could imagine them starting up again, leaving Dad all by himself in the hills of San Francisco.

My parka was down on the banister. My mittens were stuffed in its pockets. I sipped in one more stingy whiff of air, then rolled to my knees and pushed myself up. I yanked open the door to Dad's office—a loud, complaining commotion of a yank—and clomped down the steps two at a time into the land of Christmas, where twinkle lights were draping every post and column and mirror and frame. My mother had a box of tinsel in her hands. Mrs. Garland was tying velvet bows.

"So nice to see you, Mrs. Garland," I said in my I'm-so-obviously-lying voice. I pulled my parka on. I dug in for the mittens. Mrs. Garland gave me the hugest fake smile. I Cheshire Cat grinned her right back.

"Where are you going, Elisa?" my mother asked, using the tone mothers use when they're performing for their friends, when they're pretending they're the most civilized people in the world, utterly one hundred percent rational.

I had to go through the living room to get to the front door. Go around and over boxes, walk around and in between with my lungs spewed out and the air too thin for me to fill my tank. "Nowhere," I answered. "Like always." I had my hand on the doorknob. I pulled. The night air hit me like an Arctic blast, and I looked back over my shoulder at my mother, near the twinkling tree, just to see if she might call me back, but nothing. She was exchanging a look with Mrs. Garland.

"She's every ounce her father, isn't she?" I heard Mrs. Garland say as the door slammed hard behind me.

"Spitting image," I said right back. "SPITTING IMAGE!" Knowing no one would hear me, knowing they were just going to go on and on, tacking tinsel to the ceiling, rehearsing the latest psycho-science on men.

Outside, the moon seemed pushed forward in the sky, like it was looking for some kind of attention. In Mrs. Gunn's yard the noses on three hooked-together Frosty the Snowmen blinked on and off, turning the old snow to rust with the reflections, and the white plastic candles in the windows at Mrs. Garland's looked heatless and garish at the same time. In the lowest fraction of the sky the air was the color of glow.

But in the woods, except for the moon and the big spill of stars, everything was darkness. Making and roaring, I thought. Making and roaring.

20

I NEEDED THE SCORCH of the moon and the cold on my face. I needed the stream beneath the moon and the sky full of stars. I needed ravens if there were still ravens clumped up in those trees, and if there were an owl hiding out somewhere, just one white owl, I'd climb his back and I would say, Please. Fly me anywhere. *Dear Dad, I can't keep track of the changes alone, I can't do this without you. Dear Dad, it snows, then the snow is gone, then it snows again harder, and I can't find where I was going to inside all the weather. Dear Dad, Is this what it takes to be so good at poems, that you*

hurt all the time and you don't have real friends and
you have no one to talk to, so you write?

When I got to the clearing at the pond, I pulled
to a stop. For when I got to the clearing, he was
there—sitting there, on the edge of my dock, his
own kind of statue.

I almost turned. I almost slipped back into the
woods, but in the other direction were the accusing snowmen and the twinkle lights and Mrs.
Garland and my mom and all that they'd already
said and were going to say, whether I'd be there to
hear it or not, and Jilly. And between him and me
there was snow slicked over to ice and little bird
tracks and weedy trees with their limbs swooped
down, and at the end of that, the abandoned
shack, where my mother's old skates hung. I
walked the whole curving distance as if he weren't
there, as if I weren't glad to see him. I slung the
skates over my shoulder and went right out to the
end of the dock, like I always do, because the place
is mine, because no one can take it from me,

because I hadn't asked him to come again, because I had not wanted to hope.

"*Hockey* skates?" is what I said when I got to where he was. "*Hockey?* Those things don't even have toe picks." I sat down, but not near him. I took off my shoes, and over a pair of extra socks, I started lacing up, and because he wasn't going to know how I felt, or that I was glad to see him, I kept my head down, close to my heart, which was beating louder than the drums at football games, which means my rib cage, still, was puny.

"Better than boots," he finally said, pulling his cap down. "My uncle had extras." He turned and looked at me strangely, like maybe he all of a sudden wished he hadn't come or he'd remembered me differently, or maybe it was that I looked funny from all that crying I hoped he wouldn't notice I had done. It was cold, and our breath made frosty *O*s. When a twig snapped out in the woods, it sounded like something popping off. The moon was a thousand different colors, not just white. It had purple running through it, also pink.

"Moon is fat tonight," I said, after a while.

"You ever quit making poems?" he said.

"That was no poem," I told him, shaking my head. "Just a point of fact."

It's guys like Theo who could use their own Book of Words, I thought in the big yawn of nothing that followed. *Perplexing* would be a good word for him. *Variable. Mystifying.* Lila's Theo, but not. What goes on in that head of yours? I almost said, but the urge came and went, because something else that Dad taught me once is that sometimes there's nothing worse you can do to a moment than show who's better than who, and because in that particular moment after that particular day I wasn't better than anyone. I was just this lonely girl from school.

"This really your own private pond?" Theo asked, after some more undecided time had passed. He turned and looked at me, and when he did, he got slivers of moon bits in his eyes.

"Maybe," I said. Then: "Not really." My mother

and Mrs. Garland seemed whole countries away. My dad seemed close as the maybe owl.

"You mind losing a race to a guy on hockey skates?" he asked right then. Extremely stupid question.

"Get real, Theo," I said. "I'd never lose to any guy"—and that was it, it was all over, no more sitting and figuring out the conversation. Before I could finish my newest declaration of superiority, Theo was down off the dock, on the ice. He was skating away in that sloppy hockey-skater style—all noise and knees and elbows, that swish-swish-on-the-verge-of-falling sound, his butt way out, his shoulders forward. He was cutting the ice like an amateur, gaining speed by some bizarre mix of accident and luck.

"That's real big of you," I shouted after him. "You have to cheat like that to win?"

"You've got to be good for more than poems, twirl girl," Theo called from all the way across the pond. "This is the *real* world!"

"Can you do crossovers like this?" I called right back. "Can you lunge?" I was throwing all my fanciest tricks. I was weaving in circles but I was coming right at him, too, and when I got real close, he laughed at me and ducked.

"Girl stuff!" he said, pushing off now the other way, going back to where we'd come from, his elbows loose and pumping. "Why would I even want to try?" There were twigs that he was skating over. There were insect wings. There were ruts. There was everything that should have sent him sprawling, down on his face in the night. But it was my blade that hit some leaf just then, some unlucky twisting-up rut, and in that instant I was down on my knees, and then down on my butt, and that was that: I was laughing. I was laughing so hard you might have thought I was crying, but I checked, and I was laughing all right.

"Something funny?" Theo said. He was all the way across the pond, his toothy smirk like a bright white light. He was facing me, but he was skating backward toward a knot of trees.

"You," I said. "What else?" Because when he fell,

he fell like slow motion—his arms windmilling out and his feet slipping from underneath, but not all at once. One side of him was down before the other side was. When he tried to catch his balance, he went splat. "That was on purpose," he said, lying face-to-the-stars on the pond. "It's my signature move—the Theo Moses."

I was already up and coming for him, riding the diagonal in his direction, teeing to one of those very smart stops that makes a soft white shower of snow. "Hockey skates," I said when I reached him. "No toe picks. What did I tell you?" I was standing above him, in perfect girl balance. I put out my hand. "Need some help there?" I asked.

"Not on your life," he said.

"Not like it matters to me," I said. I crossed my arms and stood there watching while he made a whole lot of preposterous efforts to get up off the ice. Every time he was almost up, he was down again—on his hands and knees, or on both knees, or with his butt stuck out, or something. He looked like a beetle on its back, or like a flower dropping petals. "You could stay there until spring, and swim back," I said.

I untied my arms and stuck my toe pick in. I reached and he laughed and reached back, wrapping his gloved hands hard around my mittens, almost pulling me down, but instead I pulled him close, and he looked at me, and I was surprised, and I looked at him and felt a jolt of yearning—yes, yearning—and then he was gone, skating his hideous, jangling, hockey way back toward the dock, his crooked legs sliding out to the side, his elbows everywhere. I took my time to get to where he was, throwing a waltz jump in for good measure, turning out my feet for a spread eagle, cutting crossovers to the opposite side of the pond and performing one long (but very shaky) spiral. By the time I was ready to take off my own skates, the moon was in a different place in the sky and had lost most of its colors.

We walked back through the woods, by the

stream, where the ground sloped uphill in places and you could only wonder what was in the shadows or in the naked branches of the trees. Maybe an owl, Theo said, was near, or maybe a bear or a coyote, but Theo didn't know those woods like I knew those woods and like the woods knew me. I told Theo some of what I knew. I told him a little about my dad. I told him that I loved the line "making and roaring." But I didn't tell him about the Book of Words, and I didn't say a word about Lila, because if I didn't mention her, she wasn't there.

It wasn't until we could see the low Christmas glow of the cul-de-sac beyond the trees that we ran out of things to say, and all there was then was the sound of our boots in the snow, the snapping of twigs somewhere beyond, my mother and Mrs. Garland waiting, school tomorrow, Lila. Theo's uncle's skates danced on Theo's right shoulder. The moon caught the silver circle at his ear. There were places on the path where we couldn't walk side by side, and when that was the case, I let Theo walk ahead, until the end when he said, "No. Ladies first." Touching his hands to that place above my hips. Keeping his hands there. I walked more and more slowly. I did not want to move at all.

And that was when I saw the footprints in the snow—one footprint after another, little toes to little heels. They were leading toward the stream and then away from the stream and out, toward distant trees, like a pair of bare baby feet. When I saw them, I stopped completely, and Theo stopped right up against me, his chin above my shoulder, his skate nudging into my sleeve, his warm breath on my cool cheek, my whole self braced by him. "Look at that," I said about the little waddle shapes, and in my head I got this picture of somebody's naked baby making some kind of mad escape, a baby out running through the snow, while in my chest, I felt my heart pounding, pounding: *Kiss me, Theo. Please.* Maybe it's strangeness that makes for real friendship, something neither of you rightly understands, for one blink of one instant, in the brilliant, dark woods. Theo was right there, his chin above my shoulder. Theo was right there—and nothing. Nothing. Nothing is its own hard pain, a fever deep within. I had pride. I had to show that I didn't care.

"Bet you don't know what that is," I said at last.

"Snow angel?" he guessed, so he couldn't be wrong, but his voice was funny, tied up on itself.

"Raccoon," I said, and he kind of breathed out, then stepped away, and I kind of breathed in, but oh, it hurt. There was nothing to compare the aching to.

"You're a walking encyclopedia," Theo said, and then he pushed me and I turned and pushed him harder back, and then he called me bigheaded, and so I called him obtuse, and then I asked him, "Do you even know what that means? Obtuse," I said, "obtuse, obtuse," and we were running between the trees, after each other, away from the cul-de-sac, beneath the moon. We were running.

O NCE I HELD A BABY BIRD, but it was
dying.

I had been climbing the old pink dogwood tree
and I had seen it from above—lying on its side in
the strawberry patch. "I found a bird, I found a
bird, I found a bird," I yelled real loud to anyone
who'd listen, but I guess it was only a half-born
bird, with a head too big for its skinny neck and
wings like sacks, eyes as blind as blisters. I slid down
the dogwood tree and ran to where it was and bent
to take a closer look and then, so very gently, slowly,
I kneeled down to the ground. It looked so soft, the

bird, like it had no weight at all. It looked like all it needed was a cradle.

"I found a bird," I told the world. "I found a baby bird!" I proclaimed. And scooped it up and ran inside and opened my hands for the big world to see.

Jilly was on the couch with one of my mother's magazines—long and lovely even then, already keen on the fashions. "That is so disgusting," she said, lifting her head. "You should have been a boy, Elisa."

"Honey. Please. You take that back outside," said my mother. "It isn't sanitary." She was in the kitchen, making cookies. She raised one hand like a caution cop and pointed at the door. "You have no idea where that bird has been. You need to wash your hands."

"It's my bird," I declared to them both. "My bird!" Sticking my tongue out at Jilly and running straight past my mother and flying up the stairs, keeping the bird safe and living in the cradle of my hands. Maybe I was only six, but I was one hundred percent sure that that bird needed a bed, needed a pillow, and that my mother's pillow was the biggest of all, and therefore the very best. I grabbed her pillow from her bed. I tucked it under my chin and flew back down the stairs, and all that time I still held that bird in my hands; all that time it was a very living thing. In the laundry room it was warm and it smelled like soap. In the laundry room there was the sound of slosh, and that was where I made that bird its getting-better bed, right on top of the rumble of the dryer. I plumped up the pillow, and I laid the bird down inside a little soft place that I pressed out with my hand. And then I stood on my toes and I waited for that bird to grow out its feathers and stretch its wings and open its eyes so that it could see, but it did not. It just lay where I had put it and got very, very cold, and then it wouldn't move, and then it couldn't.

That night when Dad got home, he helped me bury the bird beside Mom's strawberry patch, inside an empty Barbie box. He called it honoring and he filled the box with twigs and leaves, and then he told me to lay the bird in by myself, lay it in nice, he said, for eternity, which of course I did, my face all hot with tears. Then he covered the box with a bunch of dirt and put a couple of daisies from Mom's garden on the mound. He picked me up, though I was too big for that. He carried me into the laundry room and helped me wash my hands.

That night it rained and rained and rained and rained, and the streets got full of gush, and the trees and the tops of the flowers seemed cut from their stems, and all I could think of was the bird in its box that would rise through the mud. It would slip from the cracks of its cardboard coffin and open its blister-blind eyes and not know anything about where it was, and if that was what eternal was, that was a very bad thing. I knew that it was my fault— that I had killed the bird, that I had buried it in the worst kind of drowning—and all I wanted then was to go outside and rescue the bird from the flood. I you can love too much, and when you love too much, you risk everything, but you also enter into a thing called beauty.

I didn't know when I was six what the word *risk* meant, but I never forgot what Dad told me. And after that night with Theo at the pond, after that chase through the trees, after the baby's feet that weren't, I put the word *risk* right in my Book of Words, under my epigraph, Making and Roaring. *Risk* was a word that it took some growing up to use. Risk was the beginning.

The next morning I tried to write Dear Lila notes for Theo.

Dear Lila, I wrote.

Dear Lila.

But I had nothing. Something had changed, and I couldn't help it, and the skies were threatening snow.

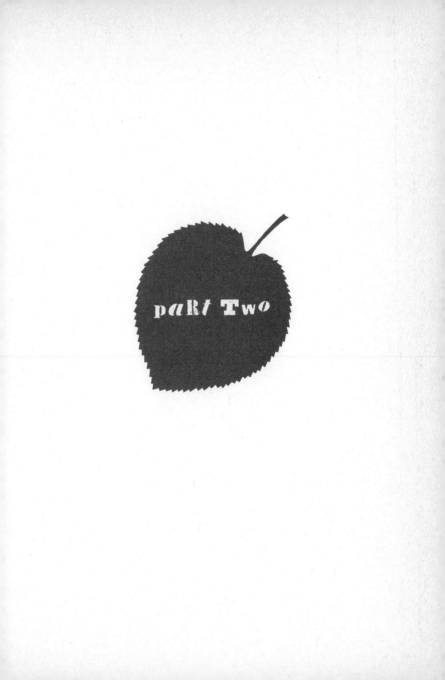

paRt Two

CHRISTMAS WAS ALWAYS my mother's holiday. She started buying gifts in March, wrapping them at night when she couldn't sleep, mentioning them briefly in passing: *Oh, I found the best thing. I can't wait until it's yours.* There was an entire room at the end of the upstairs hallway in which Mom stowed the boxes of earrings, the blouses and tights, the ties she always bought for Dad, and for as long as I could remember, Jilly and I could be trusted with that. There would have been no pleasure in ruining the surprise.

On Christmas morning we'd come downstairs,

and there would not be a place to stand. It would be as if the floor had cracked wide apart and a world of color pushed up, and through—a jagged landscape of red and white foiled boxes, snowflake cutouts, silver angel wings. On the mantel my mother would have placed birch twigs, frosted with sugar. On the windowsills she'd have arranged her Santas. And she'd be sitting there in her favorite green plush chair—her blond hair magnificently smooth, her eyes wide beneath a sky of sparkle, my dad squeezing in beside her. Christmas was my mother's holiday. It was the day of the year in which her talent for beauty was an active verb—a cascade across the room.

Dad took the red-eye home that Christmas Eve morning. A cab dropped him off. I heard it brake at the curb because I was waiting for it, because I'd been awake since so much earlier, watching the window for signs of a diminishing dark. I had a million things to tell my dad. I had as many things I knew I'd never say. But all I wanted, when I heard the cab, was to feel his arms around me, to hear him say My Littlest Girl, which is what he always called me, even after I got big.

I slid out of bed and opened the door to my room. I went halfway down the stairs and stopped. There was a pot of coffee on. There was a murmur. I understood at once that I would have to wait my turn. That some things do take precedence over a daughter's love.

They talked for the longest time, my mom and dad, but I could not make out a single word. I heard only the rise and fall of sadness and silence, the long pause and the resumption, the rush and the rebuttal. I was back in my bed with the door closed tight, watching the window, the low sun in the window, the day that was coming on strong. I heard a scuffle outside my door, the rattle of the loose doorknob turning.

"Hey." It was not my dad. It was not my mother. It was Jilly, who hadn't bothered to knock, and maybe for some sisters that would have seemed the most natural thing, but not for the two of us—

blond and auburn, pretty and not, on the opposite ends of most spectrums. She was wearing a lacy peach nightgown with cream-colored sleeves, the sort of thing I'd have thought would be worn to a party. I was wearing a T-shirt and cotton sweatpants. My hair was electrical.

"They're talking," I said, for she was studying me, saying nothing.

"I know," Jilly answered. She sighed.

"He'll probably come to see us soon."

"Maybe," she said. Then: "Do you mind?"

I didn't answer. She turned and sat on the edge of my bed. Sat there in silence, facing the window.

"Doesn't look like snow," I said.

"No," she said. "It doesn't."

And that was all between the two of us, because anything that might have been said should not have been said. Not then. It was too scary.

I woke to the sound of a slight tapping at the door. "Honey?" Dad said. "Can I come in?" I must have fallen back asleep, and Jilly, too, curled up in one corner of my bed like a cat, her long hair over her fine shoulders. "Daddy!" Jilly said, which is what she called him still, and I said, "Hey. Dad. Welcome home," putting my hands to my hair to power it down, swallowing the stale taste from my mouth. He looked faded and creased around the eyes, with a line of worry down his forehead. His hair seemed flat and lifeless. He wore an untied tie around his neck like a scarf. His pockets jingled with spare coins.

"You don't know how I've missed you," he said, coming toward us, sitting between us on my bed— his light, lithe daughter on one side, me on the other, all of us wrecked by some variant of sleep: too much, too little, our eyes a little tilted in our heads.

"Did you get my letters?" I said, though I knew he had.

"Of course."

"Did you go to Gump's?" Jilly asked.

"Without a doubt."

"How long are you home for?" I wanted to know.

"Not long enough," he said. "Never long enough."

He told us stories, then, about Stuart Small. He took us on a tour of San Francisco. He told us about the Christmas tree down on the wharf, which was taller, he said, than most anything. Then he wanted to know all about us, and Jilly told him about driver's ed and the total barf head who was its teacher, and I said only that I'd been writing poems, and maybe I could show him later, except that they were works in progress, and he said he'd like that very much, and that works in progress always had more flavor than anything perfect enough to be called finished.

"I bet you're tired, Dad," I said, and he said he was, and I took my arm from around his neck and Jilly took her arm back, too, so that he could stand and lean in and kiss us both on the forehead, then go off down the hall, to the master bedroom. Jilly was gone just as soon as he was. I lay down on my pillow and listened long as the house slowly went silent.

I KNEW THINGS were different Christmas morning when I did not hear Bing Cosby's voice floating up the stairs. When I woke and it was strangely still. Sometimes a bed is an island in a house where there's been trouble, and I did not know, lying there alone, whether the others were awake with their own wondering thoughts, or still asleep and dreaming. I did not even know what time it was, but that didn't seem to matter. An odd bleached sun pressed up against my bedroom windows, and all about the windows, like delicate frames, white webs of frost had settled in.

It took a long time before I heard anybody stir, before I felt I could go downstairs and join the day. All the twinkle lights were on, but they seemed to twinkle sadly. There were boxes wrapped in foils, but it was my dad who had come downstairs first, not my mother. He had made his way to the kitchen, pulled a big pot out of the lazy Susan cabinet, and now he was filling it with two-percent, sprinkling powdered chocolate in, heating a burner on the stove.

"Hot chocolate," he said.

I said, "Sounds good."

"We're out of marshmallows, aren't we?" He was preoccupied. The line down his forehead was a gulley, dividing left from right, before from now.

"Dad?" I said.

"Honey?" He had turned and had his back to me, was hunting through a drawer for a wooden spoon, which wasn't where he remembered it being because weeks ago Mom had moved the wooden spoons, put them in the old yellow pitcher that sat on the opposite side of the counter. I went to the pitcher. I selected a spoon. I tapped him on the shoulder.

"Merry Christmas," I said.

At last he stopped and turned to me. "Of course," he said. "Merry Christmas." And then he took me into his arms and hugged me so hard that the big white button of his light-blue pajamas pressed a circle into my cheek. "How are you doing, Elisa?" he said. "Really doing?"

But where, I wondered, do I begin? And how long was he staying this time? And did I want to weigh him down with Theo and Lila and Cyrano when he already had so much worry on his mind?

"I'm good, Dad," I said. "Just glad you're home."

We didn't open our presents until after lunch that day, and when Mom sat in her green plush chair, she sat there alone, quietly reading the tags on the boxes, summoning us to her, gift by gift. Jilly and I tried to cheer her up by trying on the gifts she'd given, until Jilly was all decked out in two sheer blouses and a red wool jacket over a new striped, slinky dress (a beret on her head, a headband beneath the beret, glass-drop earrings on her ears), and I was wrapped up like a snowman zombie in sweaters and a scarf, a pair of mittens over gloves, a fine pen my mother called "the writing pen" in my new white parka's pocket.

"You look nice, girls," is what my mother said, but looking ridiculous had been the point, and we grew louder and louder, sillier and more strange, because we wanted to make her smile, wanted to break through to the other side of this faraway place that she was in. Dad gave me a box of Ghirardelli's chocolate and a book on Alcatraz. He'd bought a pair of beaded bracelets for Jilly. There were big bowed boxes from Gump's with Mom's name on them, but she refused to open them. She wouldn't look at Dad, and once she said, as if to no one, "You have no idea how hard this has been."

"Tina," Dad said. "It's Christmas, honey. *Christmas.*"

"Well, I guess you should have thought of that," she said, "before you made your plans."

"It's not my choice," Dad said, "leaving tomorrow."

"Of course it's your choice," Mom said. "How in the world does Stuart Small rank higher than your family?"

"Tina," Dad said.

"Please," she said. "Don't." She stood and went to the kitchen. She pulled out all the makings of dinner. The turkey she'd roast and dribble with gravy. The sweet potatoes for the pie. The asparagus she'd peel and top with crushed almonds. The bags of peas and carrots. The raisin bread with the white icing that she'd made the week before. It takes a long time to make a Christmas dinner. It takes knives and bowls and pots and pans and basting brushes and metal whisks and things neither you nor I would ever think of. Mom wanted no help—not that Christmas, not that dinner—though sometimes over the course of those too many hours, I would offer, or Jilly would, or we would approach Mom together.

Mom hardly talked to Dad the rest of the day—not over dinner, not after dinner, not when Dad lit the logs in the fireplace and we all sat around the orange flames. But that night I heard them talking, talking—my mother's voice unnerving and low, my father's voice growing hard, perfunctory, explaining. Very late, he came into my room. I was wide-awake, watching the moon.

"You really leaving again?" I asked.

"I have to," he said.

"And then you're coming back?"

"That's the plan."

"Stuart Small doesn't deserve you," I said.

He ran his hand through my hair, like he used to when he would read to me at night, or just before he would set off for one of his trips across the ocean, or just after he'd found a treasure for my Stash O' Nature box. Then he reached into his pocket and pulled out something gold and bright—the shimmer of a star looped through with a midnight-colored ribbon. "I found this for you," he said, "in San Francisco." Standing, he hung the star from the lock of my nearest window. It swayed for a little while, then stopped and held its own place in the sky. "I love you lots," he said, "and don't forget it." He leaned in and kissed me right between my two wet eyes.

In the morning he was gone.

3

I GOT A FEVER, then, and I couldn't leave my bed. I couldn't turn, I couldn't talk, I couldn't see except for swirls.

If I lay perfectly still, I wasn't dead, but if I moved a single fraction of one microscopic inch, my brain did a giant lava slide and I had to concentrate very hard, else I'd fall right off my bed. If I breathed too deeply, I'd drown with air. If I thought of anything at all, I'd get ship-on-stormy-waters sick.

Time wasn't real, so time didn't pass, but for every once in a smoggy while, when I felt my

mother's hand on my flaming head or could see Jilly
sliding in through my door with a bottle of pink
aspirin in her hand, and a glass of juice, and something like worry on her face. Somebody I didn't rec-
ognize asked questions I couldn't answer, and then
I slept, and then I woke up again because something shut or something snapped, and when that
happened it was like bullets going off, bullets being
shot straight through my head, and then I crawled
to the bathroom, or it felt like crawling, I don't
know which. And then I climbed back into my bed.
Ever have all the shapes and all the colors in the
universe collide? Ever know that your head has
become a giant black hole, even though you can't
remember what Mr. Sheepals said a black hole is?

Could have been hours, could have been days.
Don't ask me; I was sick. I was sick for what seemed
such a long time that, when finally I opened my
eyes again, I saw through my window that new
snow had come—tall piles of it on the telephone
wires, high drifts on the roofs of the Garlands' and

the Blockleys'. It was as if the world were wrapped up in white cotton candy, and there wasn't any sound except the sound in the white webbing of sound—the garble of the downstairs TV, the far-away whistle of Mom's teapot, a bird in the yard, a tree limb groaning. My T-shirt felt stiff as cardboard against my skin, and my sheets were stiff, too. My hair was knots and toilet-brush bristles.

I was silly putty, spineless. I tried to fold my pillow into an *S* and to sit up halfway, but that was harder than Olympic weight lifting, and when I woke again it was dark, and someone had plugged a night-light in, put another glass of juice on my nightstand. There was a thick leather bracelet of jingle bells with a note saying *Ring me if you're hungry*, but I couldn't have lifted that thing even if lifting it would win me a million dollars, so I closed my eyes, and I dreamed that the house was falling down to dust, the house was raining down. Rafter and plank and every nail and every pantry shelf, and the books, and the pink insulating hair that may or may not have been asbestos. Then I dreamed that the mind was the moon's first word, and then it was morning and there was a star instead of the sun, and then the star hung by a strand.

When I opened my eyes again, there was Mom at the edge of my bed, her creamy hand against my forehead. "Elisa," she said, "you have to eat something."

"I can't do that." My tongue was stuck to the roof of my mouth. My words formed limp and fuzzy.

"You have to," she insisted. "It's been two days."

"What happened?" I managed.

"You've been sick," she said. "A very high fever, but it's broken. Dr. John was here, and he said you'll be fine, but you have to eat. You have to drink; you're dehydrated."

"Dr. John was here?"

"He was doing me a favor." She pulled her hand away from my forehead and handed me the plate of toast that she'd brought with her. "That's honey and butter," she told me. "It'll help."

The plate felt heavy as bricks, and my eyes were playing blur-her tricks on Mom in her red-and-green sweater, her pair of black wool slacks. She'd pulled one side of her pale hair back and put it in a clip, and I thought right then, despite everything, how pretty she absolutely was, and how there'd never been a bit of resemblance between us. I couldn't look into her and see me, and I guess things were the same from her perspective, and probably that's where the trouble between us lived, or at least where it had started.

"Where's Jilly?" I asked her.

"Downstairs, Elisa."

"What's she doing?"

"She's reading." She crossed her arms to show she was serious. "Honey," she said, "is as good as medicine."

She'd sliced the toast into four triangular pieces. I pinched the smallest slice between my fingers. My mouth felt hot and gluey inside. The toast was strange and sweet. I hate the sound you make when you're chewing and swallowing, and you're the only one for miles who is.

"There's a fresh T-shirt and pair of sweatpants at the end of your bed," Mom told me, after she'd stood there and watched me force three toast triangles in, some swallows of juice, which must have taken a week or two. "You'd probably feel better if you changed." She slipped the almost-empty plate out of my hand and picked up the glass of sipped-at juice. She headed for the door, then turned. "You ring the jingle bells if you want anything," she said.

"Thanks," I said.

"Now get some rest." She closed the door behind her with one slippered foot. I could hear the downstairs TV go loud and grow soft again, and I could hear Jilly talking, and I could feel my heart grow envious of whatever they were saying. If I turned, which I did, I could see my neon clock: 5:38 and all darkness outside. Only a wedge of moon in the sky, and the constant shimmer of a star.

THE FIRST FEW DAYS of January I stayed home from school. Dr. John said that I'd had a scare and that I needed time to get strong, and he told Mom to make a pot of chicken soup and a tray of cherry Jell-O cubes and to let me sleep however much. I still had weird rubber legs, and when I came downstairs each day, I came downstairs for good—curled myself up in front of daytime TV and let my mind go whirring. Mom insisted on keeping the Christmas lights on, and they throbbed worse than a headache, on and off and on and off, and then the chase of white to gold

That's all I knew, but I also knew this: That it was taking Mom a long time to get dressed in the morning, and she'd started doing the simplest things with her hair, and now when the phone rang and she could see it was Mrs. Garland, she just let it ring some more. More than anything, Mom just sat and stared, and still she wouldn't open the presents Dad had brought her from Gump's, which I was thinking might have helped, at least somewhat. She left them where they were, beneath the wilting tree.

Jilly brought my homework home and didn't make a scene about it, didn't even make fun of me for my messy hair. I'd already missed labs in science and the debate in social studies, and in Spanish I knew I was falling far behind. But the thing I minded missing most was Dr. Charmin's class, where Theo was, and where they were working on poems. Because maybe poems really are just what some one person writes and one somebody else picks up to read, but you still have to find the line between the two. You still have to imagine the lonesome place the poem begins and how it wants to be remembered, and all I got in the packets Jilly carried home were the poems, and not the explanations, not the stuff Dr. Charmin knew and I could not. There was a poem about a thought fox. A poem about eating poems. A poem called "Notes on the Art of Poetry," where words were sandstorms and ice blasts and things you had to believe went splash, and I needed Dr. Charmin to help me. On the fifth day of my absence there was a poem of our own we had to write—a poem about what a poem is, as best as I could tell.

"Is Archibald MacLeish telling the truth when he writes that a poem is 'palpable and mute'?" Dr. Charmin's instructions read. "Is it 'Silent as the sleeve-worn stone / Of casement ledges where the moss has grown'? Can a poem be *wordless*? What is a poem? What can a poem be?"

"Mom," I said, "can we turn off the TV?"

"Won't it be good"—she sighed—"when you're all the way well?"

That night we had chicken soup for dinner, and I sat at the table since I was well enough for that. Mom and Jilly talked about a show they watched on TV, guessing what would happen to their favorite characters as if they were next-door neighbors or people you could call up on the phone. Mom had turned down the kitchen lights and lit a candle, to celebrate, she said, my getting off the couch, and I wished I wasn't wearing sweatpants and an old sweatshirt, because Mom had put her fake-pearl necklace on and Jilly had all her earrings in—four on one side, three on the other. This was their conspiracy—they were trying. Anyone looking in on us would have thought I was the guest of a pretty people's family. But they wouldn't have guessed that my mother's heart was broken. That she was putting on a show so none of us would get sick again with missing Dad or worry.

The flame of the candle had sunk deep into the wax. Outside, the fallen snow had started blowing, and it looked like more white stuff was coming. Jilly was talking about a pair of boots she had seen in the mall that was finally on sale, and Mom was saying that they could go tomorrow after school and see if the boots were worth what they were asking, and Jilly said, Well, then, can I drive? Because she had her permit. My thoughts were far away from boots and cars. I was trying to imagine Theo without his Lila poems, and Dad in San Francisco. I was wondering whether you really could write a poem about a poem without saying what was obvious or had been said before.

"Mom," I said, "I think I'm going up to bed."

"Okay," she said. She nodded.

Only later, after I'd turned off the lights and curled under the quilt and listened to the wind kicking around outside, did I hear Mom talking with her sister, Georgia, who lives half a world away.

"It's my fault," she was saying. "I said things I shouldn't have said. I went too far. I hurt him. I ruined Christmas. Maybe more than Christmas.

And Elisa's been sick, and did I make her sick? Is such a thing possible?"

"No, Georgia," my mother said after a pause. "That isn't it."

"No. That isn't true. I'm to blame for it, too."

"No, Georgia, this isn't helping me. I love him, see? I blew it."

Then I didn't hear my mother saying anything at all, only the sound of her sobbing, then the sound of Jilly's "Mom?" And then the star in my window shuddered, as a cold wind blew through the night.

T HERE'S A MIRROR in my parents' room that runs floor full up to ceiling, and that's where Mom has always gone to verify which colors are becoming. When I was little and knew nothing about what qualified for beauty, I'd sit on my parents' bed with Jilly and watch her get dressed for Friday nights. Over her sheeny slip she'd zipper dresses. With her long, skinny fingers she'd fix her hair. She would put slightly gray shoes with slightly blue blouses and dark, mysterious skirts, and Jilly would clap her hands and say, "Mommy, you look exactly like the weather." Standing tipped forward, toward the long mirror, Mom would draw on her eye powders and scroll her mascara, and always Dad would wait downstairs so he could see her, as he liked to say, all at once and all together. Just before she'd leave, Mom would cup one hand beneath Jilly's chin and one hand beneath mine, lift our eyes to hers, and make a promise: "Someday, girls. Someday."

Jilly was the best student Mom ever had. She knew all the secret places in Mom's closet, all the compartments in all the boxes, all the shoes in the hanging sleeves of shoes, all that was hidden behind plastic; Jilly knew lipstick. "Don't tell, Elisa," she'd say. "You have to promise"—fitting herself into one of Mom's fancy dresses and slicking it down across her hips. The silk or the cotton or the nylon would fall like water falls, spilling past Jilly all over the floor, and whatever shoes Jilly chose would be gallons too big, impossible to walk in. "Elisa, what do you think?" she'd say, and I'd say, "Jilly's beautiful," and when I said that, she'd smile like a movie star and blow me juicy kisses.

Jilly understood about prettiness—that it's not just a gift, it's a talent. That it's cracking the code of your face to find its sweetest side, doing the math regarding standing, walking, sitting, waiting. Pretty people practice pretty. They turn their gift into a talent.

That afternoon I was alone without the TV on, and nobody calling. Outside, the snow was banked high against the house but the streets were clean from plowing. Jilly and Mom had gone to the mall in search of boots, and I knew the way they shopped, the way they'd now be out for hours. Anywhere I wanted to go in the house was mine to go. Anything I wanted to do, I could. But I'd been boiled down to nothing by the fever—a pile of bones in a bunch of oversized clothes—and even my freckles seemed fainter than they'd been, and I felt old. I sat and then I roamed—an operative. I lay on my bed and then I went downstairs and ate half a box of Lorna Doones. I looked at books inside Dad's office. I scribbled words into my book of words. I went downstairs, and then I went downstairs again, to the darkness of the basement.

It's the smell of a basement that makes a basement, and that's one hundred percent of the truth. The old termite tunnels, the monster mold on ancient telephone books, the sour whatever it is that rises up from the round metal plate in the concrete floor. Dad was always too tall and light for our basement, but that meant absolutely nothing, because the basement always belonged to him. It was where he put his tools and his storage boxes, where he had his shelves filled up with treasure. I learned Stash O' Nature from Dad, who left his Nature in full display, on his hand-built wooden shelves. The tiny white skulls of moles and mice. The nest a robin had made of Christmas ribbons. The oddest collection of naked twigs. Dad was in a contest with himself to find the most outstanding twig, he said. The most perfect and unblemished of all twigs. "What do you do when you win?" I once asked him. "I start over," he replied.

On the farthest, darkest basement wall was Dad's spice rack—a black iron shelf with a little lip and a bunch of jars. He had aniseed and cardamom, juniper berry and caraway, cumin, turmeric, and mint. He had leaves and flecks of leaves and seeds— all these things he'd picked up from wherever Point of View had taken him. Dad said the spices were his memories of the places he had been, his way of keeping track, and that afternoon, alone in the house, I unscrewed the lid of every one of Dad's jars and buried my nose in the distance. He and Mom had talked late, late last night. She had hung up crying.

By the time Mom and Jilly got home, it was dark, and by then I was lying on my bed, beneath my covers, just watching the sky through my windows, the last band of pink, then the blackness. Tomorrow I'd be well enough for school, for the new year that had crept in with me hardly noticing, and there'd be Margie with her gossip, and Bolten with his nose, and every Spanish conversation I had not had and wouldn't now, for forever. There'd be Theo, who would or would not be wrapped up in Lila, Theo who would or would not have made a choice, who would or would not have been missing me. There'd be so much catching up to do, so much fitting back in, but I had changed. I wanted more than I had before, and that would make things harder.

Downstairs Jilly and Mom were murmuring about something—wrestling whatever they'd found out of bags, throwing down their purses. I pulled the covers up over my head, and the night went even darker, and their voices were more faraway, and I was floating, hovering. I don't know if time went by, or if I slept. All I know is that after that, I sensed both their faces peering down from high above my bed.

"What are you doing with the covers pulled up like that?" It was Mom who was asking. She'd had her face made over at the mall, it seemed, and the sky above her eyes was brighter. She was backlit from the hallway light and looked a lot like glow.

"You could have suffocated," Jilly said. She was standing on the opposite side of the bed from Mom, looking down like you see TV doctors do, the blondest parts of her hair coming forward, her mouth twisted with either dismay or concern; I was too foggy-eyed to tell. And then the phone rang and Jilly was sure it was for her, and she practically skipped out of the room.

"Jilly found her boots," my mother said.

"That's good." I had pushed myself up on my elbows by then, was taming the bristles of my hair with three fingers. I was looking at her face, and the subtle lift of it.

"And there was this," Mom said, "that I got for you." She was holding out one hand, then opening that hand to show her palm. Perched on its center, like some magnificent butterfly, was one of those hair clips you see the pretty girls wearing, with bits of cut glass that you could swear were jewels, and the most complicated filigree.

"You got that for me?" I said, confused.

"I did." She nodded.

I took the clip from Mom's hand and came up higher in the bed and turned it over and over, to catch the hallway light, to count the jewels and the colors of the jewels. It was the prettiest thing I'd ever seen, and I had no clue how to use it. Mom must have been reading my mind. She went down the hall, and then she came back with a mirror in one hand. "Sit up," she said, laying the mirror and the clip on my lap, and as I sat up straighter, she put her fingers in my hair, lifting it up over my *W* ear. When she had gotten whatever effect she was seeking, she picked up the clip and sunk it in. Then she stood back and assessed her work like I wasn't even there. Shaking her head, she took out the clip and started again.

"I think it needs to go higher," she said. That was all. She kept working my hair, working her fingers through my hair, placing and re-placing the clip, and then she told me to take a look, and she lifted the mirror from my lap so I could see. All of a sudden there were two of me in bed, each of us looking at the other. We saw surprise in each other's faces. We saw confusion, and wonder. "What do you think?"

"I think . . ." I said, "I think . . ." But neither of me knew what to say. Neither had a word for the moment. We were the same small mouth, the same uncommitted chin, the same sturdy nose, the same completely unexceptional cheekbones. We were the same, except there was something different. There was something lifted up in us, and not only the left side of the wild auburn hair.

"It brings out your eyes," my mother said, "is what it does."

Get Back to Me

I ran for you,
with my winter boots on
and my coat flapping open.

Of course it was cold.
Of course you were far away and I ran
Across the cul-de-sac, beside the stream,
Inside the moon's blue shadow,
The triste of the moon,
Where I thought you might be
Since I needed to find you.

I got sick afterward, and it snowed,
And there was no proof of me
Running
And there was no poem
So everything had to begin again.
Please.
Get back to me.

6

YOU ARE BORN or you're not born with a talent for hair; I came out on the loser's side. I didn't know, the next day, how to pin my hair as back and as high as my mother did, but I wore the clip nevertheless, and I wore it in my own way, because there's nothing worse than being my age and being dependent on other people for good hair. Mom said, "If you start to feel sick, call." Jilly said, "See you around." I walked out the front door, down across the yard, and over those few blocks to school.

It was hard to remember the order of things—which bell was caution, which bell was real, whether you went left with the first number on the locker dial, or spun the wheel around twice the other way. I got a woozy feeling trying to get it all right, and then that feeling passed.

The halls seemed rock-concert crowded, elbow to elbow, and the floor was that brown sludge color that floors can get after the snow outside gets old. I could see Jilly down by the water cooler showing her new boots to the fashionable crowd, and when Margie passed by, she looked at me twice, like I'd grown a fourth ear or something. "Hey, Margie," I said, but she didn't say "Hey" back. She was caught up in the crowd surge, like a leaf flushed down a river. Math, I thought. And social studies, and science. Take one thing at a time, and as it comes. My locker had that stale, needs-air smell. My pencil tips were as dull and blunt as the ends of used Magic Markers. Wire-spiraled notebooks and three-ring binders. Erasers and pens. One or another of the bells was ringing, but I couldn't tell which one. I felt someone standing close to me. I turned and it was Theo.

"Must have been some flu" is what he said.

"Fever," I said. He seemed taller to me than he had before. He'd lost the dancing monkey. His eyes looked deep into mine. There were a million people with a million backpacks knocking all around us, and something whammed me from the rear. I felt my face go hot, touched the butterfly in my hair.

"You missed a big scene in Dr. Charmin's class," Theo said, stepping out of the way of a cresting crowd surge, closer to me.

"I did?"

"She threw Sarah into after-school detention."

I laughed, grabbed the last of my things, and slammed my locker. "Serves her right," I said. "For what?"

"For reading a Dylan Thomas poem with a French accent."

"You're kidding." Theo was close. We were arm against arm. I could have reached for his hand.

How could I know—how can you tell?—if he was thinking of my hand?

"It was a riot."

We were two on a raft with the mobs and multitudes, the elbows and knuckles, the catcalls and hollers. We were friends, or were we more? I kept checking for Lila, but she wasn't there. I looked more closely at Theo. He'd changed the circle in his ear.

At the door of Mr. Marcoroon's door, I half stepped in to check out the board and all that I in my feverish spell had missed. You ever see a piece of glass after it's been shattered into pieces? That's what I saw there—all these broken bits and squiggles, triangles and letters, question marks. I saw disaster in the making. Brain chaos.

"I can't do this," I said to Theo, who had waited.

"You're a genius," he said, laughing. "Don't you remember?"

"Well, sure," I said, "compared to you." But the last bell had rung, and he was sliding away. I took my seat in Math Hell.

Auspicious is a word that means promising.

Sanguine means rosy, bright.

Craving is desire through and through—a hunger and a flame.

THAT AFTERNOON Dr. Charmin introduced the villanelle, another something French, she said, and powerful, giving Sarah a silencing look. The board had been chalked with what seemed like Greek to me—beats and syllables, paired rhymes and repetitions, the word *tercet* five times, and then the word *quatrain*. A few rows ahead of me and over, Theo was taking notes, his shoulders hunched and his back to me, but I knew I couldn't study him, because Margie was studying me. "Welcome back, Elisa," I heard Dr. Charmin saying, as if she'd just noticed I was there. "It's nice to see you looking well." You couldn't take a teacher's word for something like that: Forty-eight eyes whisked toward me and stared. Theo winked.

We were all divided then into six sets of four and given copies of a poem. "You learn villanelles by listening to villanelles," Dr. Charmin began again, as now she walked up and down the aisles, distributing the day's work. "What we're reading today is Elizabeth Bishop's masterpiece 'One Art.' If you never read another villanelle in your life, then at least you will have this one swimming in your blood. Don't try to do the poem's mathematics just yet. Just read aloud when I tell you to, and listen for the patterns.

"This group here," Dr. Charmin pointed. "Take the first tercet. And so on"—she gestured again—"as it goes."

"Like 'Row, Row, Row Your Boat' for adults," someone mumbled, though nobody, in the post-Sarah administration, even dared to laugh.

"'The art of losing isn't hard to master;'" the

designated group began, not in sync at first, then finding its stride:

> *so many things seem filled with the intent*
> *to be lost that their loss is no disaster.*

"Second tercet?" Dr. Charmin said, raising her hand like a maestro, and commanding from Sarah, Theo, Mitchell, and only-ever-gives-dumb-answers Lurch a choral-quality response:

> *Lose something every day. Accept the fluster*
> *of lost door keys, the hour badly spent.*
> *The art of losing isn't hard to master.*

Then the third tercet was brought to full voice and released, and then the fourth, and finally the fifth, which was my own, which I read with Candy, Daniel, and Hart, who sit in the back of the room hoping they'll never be noticed and made like background vocals to my solo act:

I lost two cities, lovely ones. And, vaster,
some realms I owned, two rivers, a continent.
I miss them, but it wasn't a disaster.

"The quatrain," Dr. Chamin said, and it was read, then there was silence. "It's fierce, isn't it?" she suggested. "Fierce, and also quite a surprise. You have to have something to say when you write, and Bishop says it all. What's more, she does it within the strictures of a very particular form. So what, in the end, is a villanelle?"

"Tercets and quatrains," Matt said.

"Five of the first, one of the latter." Dr. Charmin nodded. "But beyond all that, what's the pattern? Look at the poem. Which lines repeat? How are they changed, with the repeating?"

"Master and disaster," Theo said, "are the big words."

"And not just the words themselves—right, Theo?—but also the lines that they're attached to."

"Right."

"Somebody tell me how Elizabeth Bishop has taken chances."

"The last line," I said, when nobody else would, "looks like a note to self."

"What else?"

"It isn't a perfect one-hundred-percent copy of the lines it's supposed to be patterned off of."

"Which means?"

"That the meaning was fiercer than the form right there? Or that maybe you show fierceness by breaking form?"

"Interesting perspective, Elisa. Thank you."

"Are we going to have to write villanelles?" It was Margie, wanting to know.

"Of course we are. This is Honors English."

"But it looks so hard," said Candy. Sarah sighed really loudly but said nothing.

"I'm giving you the rest of the class," Dr. Charmin said, "to get started. Ask me questions, if you have them."

There was the sound, then, of paper being torn

from notebooks, of feet shuffling out, chairs being pushed back, elbows hitting desks. I stole a look at Theo, pushing the blank page around before him. Then I saw Margie watching me watch Theo. She made a face and cracked her gum.

I T USED TO BE in winter that I dreamed of summer, when I could go out and hunt all day on behalf of Stash O' Nature. Drinkable skies, I'd think of, and amber sun. Kitschy color in the garden. A little stir through an open door. The yakking of frogs. I liked darkness bowing out to light. I liked glisten on the grass, the pinkest morning. Sometimes the closest we get to being where we want to be is imagining we're already there. I used to dream of summer in winter, of hitching all my thinking to the sun.

But now it was the moon I wanted, to lamp up

my pond in the woods. The indigo shadows and the statue girl, the book she held that had no words but seemed to tell a story. Track the changes, Dad had said, and this was one: I'd become a winter girl. I'd found my variety of loveliness on a pair of stolen skates.

Jilly and Mom were out that night—Jilly with Elaine and Mom at the gardening class she took at the local community college. That left me alone and well enough to fly. To cut through the cul-de-sac and down, along the stream, between the shadows. It was a most outstanding cold, the air like ice cubes up against the skin. I could run and I could slide and I could ride the icy snow, and I was fever thin, but I didn't mind; I was back where I belonged. I kept running until I could run no more. I walked the rest of the way through the shadows to the pond, to the shack, to the dock's end. I laced the old skates on.

Do you know the musical *West Side Story*, with that white tough Tony and that Puerto Rican Maria making like Romeo and Juliet? You know that song "Somewhere," about peace and quiet and open air? "There's a place for us," it starts, the first word becoming the next word, slowly. "There's a time for us." Each note as pure as a promise.

I skated to the middle of the pond. I stood up straight. I pushed outside edge right, then outside edge left, then swept myself into the music, assembling all my speed and bending my knees. When I jumped, my speed carried me high, forward; it lifted the song right off its feet. When I landed, I made my toe picks quiet—made swish and leap my only sounds. I crossed over and over and over, then leaned back against the night, pointing my right foot east, pointing my left foot west, and drawing, just like a pencil would, a long, crisp, curving line. That was me, the girl above the pond. Me with my arms thrown out and the night behind me, the night holding me up, for that's how it's done. I was the beginning and the end, the poem I had yet to write, transcendent, which is not the same thing, not the same thing in the least, as being invisible. I was what the moon was shining its spotlight on.

Words for the future:

Seraph, which is an angel of the highest echelon.

Sylph, which is the thing that rides the breeze.

Empyreal, which is of the sky, which is also, without question, sublime.

Diaphanous, which is a way of saying faint, transparent, slight.

Superlative, which is top-notch stuff, the most expensive brand.

Limned, which is what you'll be when the moon looks down as you skate alone in winter.

"Somewhere" is a song. It is a pond, at night.

ONCE I SAW A PICTURE of Mom and Dad together on the day they bought the house we live in now. They were sitting on the stoop, knee to knee—Mom's long yellow skirt warm and buttering to the ground, her collar tips all purple pansied; that was when my mother sewed, when all her clothes were, as she liked to say, stunning originals. A thin black band held back her corn-silk hair, and there were diamonds in her ear-lobes. Dad was wearing a short-sleeved shirt and khaki pants with a crease down each leg, but he was still looking at Mom like he was surprised to find her on the stoop right next to him. My mother had taken her tall-heeled sandals off and tossed some daisy stems across her yellow lap. Dad did not wear glasses yet. In his hand was a bowl of strawberries, fresh picked from the patch out back.

In that picture of my parents, it is just the two of them—the front door black because Dad had not yet varnished it dark green, the old pots of begonias without their cracks, the hanging plaque—ONE HOUSE ONE HOME—still sitting on a barrel at that antique store where my parents would, as the story went, find it, claim it, bring it back, and nail it to their castle. I could never figure how that photograph of my parents came to be—who came close enough to their private world to steal a glimpse like that.

By the time I got home from the pond that night, Mom and Jilly were back from where they both had been. Their coats were thrown over the banister, and on the stairs they sat—Jilly two steps above Mom with one fist on one knee, her chin in the nest of that fist. They'd been talking, I guess, but now they weren't, or there I was, so they had stopped. "Hey," Jilly said, and I said, "Hey." "Where were you?" my mother asked, and I said, "Walking," and she didn't ask where or why. "Come here," she said instead, in a way that made me understand she was not mad, just tired.

I pulled off my Christmas mittens, my Christmas parka, my Christmas scarf, my boots. I rolled up the cuffs of my snow-crusted jeans. In my thick white socks I skated across the floor of the wide beginning of our house, which isn't really a hallway but has never been a room. Jilly lifted her chin from her fist, then put it down again. Mom wrapped one piece of her blond, blond hair around her longest finger. I knew, and I guess they knew I knew: Dad had called and there'd been another fight. Things were getting harder now, more scary. There was room for me on a step below. I took my place, beneath them.

So we sat that way, the three Cantor girls, in the house my parents had bought when they were young. And even though you can't remember what you were not born in time to see, I was thinking how it must have been—my parents harvesting the strawberry patch, my mother saying yes to daisies, my father amazed by the butter of the skirt that melted past Mom's knees. I was thinking of the house before me, of time before I knew it, of Dad when he loved my mom so much that he would stand at the bottom of the steps imagining her beauty. I don't know yet if beauty exists if there's no one there to see it, but I know this: My mom needed Dad to see her now. To pick strawberries for her in winter.

In an hour we would all take every inch of Christmas down—the twinkle lights, the indoor wreaths, the ornaments hooked on the knobby tree. We would box up the Santas and the frosted birch twigs and untie all the bows and stuff the tinsel into a Ziploc bag in case we needed it next year. We would put away the jingle bells and the snowflake lamps and every last holly-and-mistletoe runner.

Fox-Trot

By the stream the fox and she-fox stood
Nose to nose beneath the stars
Dancing the music of the woods.

The deer rapped a beat with their hooves,
The ravens sang from raven hearts
As by the stream the fox and she-fox stood.

The great owl called as a great owl would,
The squirrels all shimmied in the dark,
Dancing the music of the woods.

Then from the north a fierce wind blew
And broke the starry dance apart
By the stream where the fox and she-fox
stood.

The ravens flew as ravens would,
Deer ran off, squirrels scuttled far
Away from the music of the woods.

The stars blinked out, also the moon.
The air went silent, cold, and hard
By the stream where the fox and the
  she-fox stood
Dancing the music of the woods.

10

THE NEXT MORNING Theo was at my locker with the twitchiest look on his face—maybe nerves, maybe excitement, I couldn't tell and there wasn't time to tell, because the morning rush had started. All the elbows, knuckles, knees again, the pitches and swishes of talk that smashed against metal, vinyl, and ceiling tile and got all mucked up into the din.

"What's up?" I asked when I finally cut through the crowd and got to Theo, who slid one locker down and crossed his arms but otherwise went nowhere.

"Hey" is all he said.

I combo'd the locker dial. Thirty-six. Nineteen. Two. I kneeled in close and collected my books and collected my pens and found the red pencil I would need for Mr. Marcoroon's class and took off my coat and hung it on the hook and stood back up and slammed the door, and all that time Theo stood there, nervous. For all I knew Lila's bus was rolling in. Or Bolten was hanging back, spying. Something.

Theo's shirt was only half tucked into his jeans. He had a leather string around his neck and no earring I could see because his hair had grown that long, and even though Dad says that you've always got to watch your pride, I felt a little jolt of pride when I turned and Theo joined me down the hall. I touched my hair, I checked my jeans, I looked down at my turtleneck and I suppose I was presentable, but I wasn't Lila, I wasn't lovely, I wasn't Theo's girlfriend: What was I, then, to him?

"I have something," Theo said above the noise. "To show you."

"And that would be what?" I asked. We'd reached hallway number two. We'd turned. I looked at him but could read nothing on his face, nothing in his cobalt eyes.

"I didn't mean right now," Theo said. "You going to the pond? After school?"

"Can't you just tell me what it is?" I asked. "I mean—" We'd reached Mr. Marcoroon's class, and the bell was blaring, and I had to know; I could not wait. I looked hard at him. His eyes held mine. I felt my stomach turn.

"I'm not telling you anything," Theo said. "Pond or no pond? Your choice." He had this glimmer in his eye. This something happy that I had not fully seen, not even at the pond, when we were skating.

"You joining us today, Miss Cantor?" Mr. Marcoroon called from the front of his room.

"Looks like you're wanted," Theo said. "So what will it be?"

"You've got to tell me what it is," I said.

"Not going to happen," Theo said. "Not here." He was so full of—what? Anticipation, I guess. He was so full of happy anticipation.

"Okay," I said. "Okay. Whatever."

He touched his finger to my cheek. He said, "Well, that's good."

"Theo?" I said.

"What?" I wanted to touch him back. I wanted to reach for him.

"Oh my God," I said.

"What?"

"It's Lila," I said. For it was true. Her bus had rolled in. She was headed for us—clomping down the hallway in a pair of killer boots.

"Leave him alone," she said when she reached the door to Mr. Marcoroon's room.

"We're just talking," I said.

"Really?" she said. And she reached for me. Lifted her hand to me. Seemed just this close to giving my face a good, hard slap.

"Don't touch her," Theo said to Lila.

"Don't you talk to me, Theo. Not a word."

The bell was ringing. He took her hand. They walked away from me.

Ignominy.
Denigrated.
Desolate.

You know what they mean.

11

I GOT TO THE POND as early after school as I could, after calling up to Mom, who was behind her bedroom door, that I'd see her in a while. I'd messed with my hair and clipped up the one side, and I'd stolen a tube of Jilly's lipstick, some frosty peaches stuff that I smeared, then smackered on. The sun was low and skittish in the sky, having broken out of the day's gray murk just an hour or so before. I knew the chances of Theo showing were slim. But I had to take the risk, didn't I? I had to have my shot at beauty.

I took my time lacing up Mom's skates, and I

took my time warming up—long strokes on the long sides of the pond, crossovers on the short parts. Every few times around I'd stop to slide the crystals off my blades, or sit on the dock to catch my breath—to wait, really; I was waiting. The sun falls awfully fast in winter, and after it falls is when the woods start snapping with sounds you would not notice in the day. *Dad,* I'd write, if I were writing to Dad, *Here's another change I've noticed: The dark is more than the sun dropping off, more than the moon and the stars. It's what you can't see that you hope you will see, what hasn't been that might be.*

I tried to imagine Dad in San Francisco, then tried to picture him talking to Stuart Small, a man who had to shave his head to elevate his stature, a man who expected loyalty from people he diminished. I tried to imagine Dad imagining me, Jilly, and Mom, imagining home, but when someone you love like that goes away that long, you can't know that he's the person he once was. *Dear Dad,* I'd write, if I were writing to Dad, *How can you stay*

and over in the center it was smooth and polished as a tabletop, a perfect white sky for the marble girl who was still, I imagined, reading her book. Still studying the same blank page in anticipation of some story sweetly delivered, or some one phrase. How long that girl had waited, I thought. How silent it must be, inside the ice. How enduring you have to be to take one day, and then the next. Here is a word, if you are looking for one: **Interregnum**, which means a pause, a gap, the long held note between two things. That's what that afternoon was.

Theo wasn't coming. I looked out into the woods, I listened, I could tell. He'd asked to show me something, and I had said yes, and now he wasn't here and I'd never know what might have been.

T HE NEXT MORNING I asked Mom if she could clip my hair high and pretty as she had on the night she'd come home with Jilly from the mall. I had to knock on her door, because she hadn't left her bed since the night before, when Jilly had taken her a bowl of cereal and a chocolate bar for dinner. "She's really sad," Jilly had said to me, and I'd said, "I know," and that night I stayed downstairs with Jilly, watching her soaps on TV, eating grocery-store popcorn and the last four pieces of cheese Danish in an Entenmann's box.

"What are we going to do?" I asked.

"It's up to Dad to come home," Jilly said. "We're already here."

In the morning Mom sat in the center of her queen-size bed, which made her look distant and small. The lace part of the curtains was drawn across her windows, with the purple velvet heavy part hanging bunched and vertical. A single night-stand lamp burned beneath a beige-ish hat-shaped shade. Mom was wearing a long-sleeved white T-shirt, loose white drawstring pants, and an old white terry-cloth robe that she had not bothered to tie closed. She wore nothing on her hands but the big round diamond ring that Dad had given her years ago, before either of them could see as far ahead as Jilly or me, Point of View, Stuart Small in San Francisco. Her hair was slept-on hair, damp-looking and flat, and she had painted no lines of color around her eyes, no patches of blush on her cheekbones, so her eyes seemed smaller, and they were lumpy, too, with crying, and her sheets were white—did I mention that?—and also her quilts and her pillows. "Jilly?" she'd asked, when I'd knocked, and I'd said, "No, Mom, it's me," and when I opened the door, then closed it, I saw her twice, one in the bed, the way she was, and once in the long, bright mirror.

"I can't make it look the way you make it look," I told her, holding the butterfly clip in the palm of one hand and opening it up so she might see.

"It's just pulling your hair back and lifting it high," she said. "It's simple, Elisa. Really."

"But better when you do it," I told her, and she looked at me, her wild-haired daughter, and very slowly sighed. I stood beside her bed. She did not raise her hands. "It's going to be another cold day," I said, and she said, "Aren't they all, anymore?" I said, "Can I sit here?" I smoothed a hand across her bed, and because she didn't say no, I did.

"Tired?" I asked.

"Terribly so," she said.

"Dad'll come back, Mom," I said. "He has to."

"Oh." She reached for my hand with her hand.

"Everything Dad has is here," I said. "I mean—everything, don't you think? His tools and his spices and shelves of Nature, that place downstairs where he stands waiting for you? The strawberry patch and me and Jilly—"

"I've made him unhappy, Elisa, and that matters, too. He sounded so far away last night." She looked at me as if I'd never understand, and maybe if I'd mentioned Theo just then, she would have known that I know about hurting, I was a new expert on the subject. Except that ruining something that hasn't really begun is not as bad as messing with a marriage, and also, if I told Mom the Theo story, I'd have to explain about Cyrano and also make confession about the pond through the trees, in the dark. That was just too much; I couldn't. Besides, the only one who could have helped Mom just then was Dad.

"Sit down, Elisa," my mother said, and at the edge of that winter bed, I did, shifting the weight of everything, sliding Mom just a notch from the center. She gave me a long look, what I think they call a searching look, then reached her hands toward me. She combed my hair through with her pale, sad hands, lifted my hair above my good ear. I watched her work in the mirror glass. I saw the clip go in.

"You'll be late for school," she said.

"I don't mind," I told her.

"Well, I do, Elisa. You're my Honors student. I'm not going to mess that up." She combed her fingers through the rest of my hair, above my double earlobe. "If you want, I can show you how to fix this side," she said. "Tomorrow. When there's time."

That was the day that I walked with Jilly all the way to school. When we talked a little about Mom and Dad, the future. When Jilly said it must be nice to be smart, and I said it must be nice to be pretty. "Pretty doesn't get you into college," she said, and I said, "Smart doesn't get you any boyfriends." And I had meant for her to laugh, but she looked at me strangely sad instead, said, "Yeah? And how long does pretty last?" I didn't know what to say to that, so I said, "Big things down the road for you, Jilly. I see a future in fashion."

We heard the first caution bell when we were three whole blocks out. We looked at each other, shrugged. "Mr. Marcoroon is going to kill me," I said.

"I always hated him," Jilly said. "Don't you?"

THERE WERE DAYS after that when the only Theo I saw was Lila's Theo—his arm through hers, her hand up in his curls. Down the halls and around the halls they were Elmer's glued together, and I understood that he'd been forced to choose and I had not been favored. Lila had gotten her black hair cut, her bangs sheared at her nose. She had to shake her head so you could see her eyes, so she could look at you. She looked at me hard when she was standing with Theo.

In English Theo was a shell of himself—never turning my way or meeting my eyes. Even when I brushed by him on the way to my chair, even when I timed things just so that the two of us were entering or leaving at the same time, he made like we'd never really been friends. Class went on for what seemed like whole days at a time. It was pantoums, it was elegies, it was odes—Shelley, Keats, Longfellow, the big boys, Dr. Charmin called them, who were famous for things like writing about wind or pictures on a vase. It all seemed sort of dusty, dull. Regulated. Formal. I couldn't find the soul of it, or my own poet's heart. I answered when I was called upon, never volunteered. When my own ode was read aloud in class, it was about as good as Sarah's.

Out in the wider world, Mr. and Mrs. Sue were going public with their spats—eating at separate ends of the cafeteria and staring each other down, skimming down opposite sides of the halls, laughing the loud false laugh with other people. I waited for Karl to ask me for a fix; he seemed to know not to. He didn't approach me for poems, and other guys didn't, and I might as well have been wearing

weren't going to give Mom any bigger cause for sadness. We weren't going to give Dad any new excuse to stay away. We walked together in the morning, and we were the Cantor sisters in school, and you weren't going to take that away from us, even if we would never in a million years admit this to each other.

On Thursday Dr. Charmin said that I would be meeting her after school—didn't ask me, just told me that I would. I wasn't sure if I was in the mood to talk. I went to the bathroom, stood in line at the water fountain, slouched inside the door of the gymnasium to watch the guys' basketball practice. They'd made the play-offs, and they were cocky as hell, but anything was better than a lecture.

"Well here you are, Elisa," Dr. Charmin said, when I finally arrived fifteen minutes past the appointed time. She was straightening the chairs after her senior seminar, wiping some notes off the board. There was a little clap of chalk on her red wool skirt, and her hair had gotten loose again, hung in helter-skelter style around her face, making her seem younger. I wondered how she would look if she let her hair loose all the way, if she brought her weekend self to school. I wondered what she wanted. Finally it was like she'd remembered I was there. "Sit down," she said, as if I'd entered her living room. "Please." As if there'd be tea. I dropped my backpack on the floor, slipped into a front-row chair. She continued straightening, washing down the boards, sifting through some papers on her desk.

"You're not yourself, Elisa, are you?" she began. She positioned herself along the front of her desk and leaned against the protruding metal rim. She pushed her straggling hair off her forehead, tied her arms across her chest. She had a chunky ring around her middle finger, like something you'd find at a crafts fair. It occurred to me then what had been obvious all along—bad jewelry was her second passion. Big, unwieldy, complicated stuff, counterweights, I supposed, to the delicacy of stories and language. Maybe she thought no one would notice. Or maybe she hoped someone would. I couldn't tell. But she'd asked a question and she stood there waiting, and I decided I wouldn't resist, wouldn't extend, unnecessarily, the interrogation.

"I try to be," I answered.

"You're different in class, less engaged with your work, hardly as creative as I know you can be. In a nutshell, Elisa, your work is sloppy. Something's going on, and I am asking what that is."

"I'm sorry, Dr. Charmin."

"I'm not interested in apologies, Elisa."

"I'll do better," I said, raising my eyes to hers so that she would know I meant it.

"That might be true and that's important, but that isn't why I've called you here. Is it something with another student, Elisa? Is something going on at home?"

I waited.

"It's not that you have to tell me, Elisa. We both know that you don't. But I'd like to help if I can. If there's something I could do." Her whole face turned red when she said those words.

I noticed, looked away, felt embarrassed for both of us. I hated that things had gone so far as to warrant a private session with Dr. Charmin. And if she could tell that my life was a mess, what did others know, what were they saying behind their hands when I walked by? No one had bothered me for a week at least. Not even Marcoroon.

"'Fox-Trot,' Elisa. Yes? That was your last good poem."

"Okay."

"After that, it's been throwaways that anyone could do."

"I'll do better."

"Listen to your own work, Elisa. Listen to what you are capable of." She turned and rooted around the piles on her overpiled desk, until she'd found what she'd been searching for. "Fox-Trot," she said, then read the villanelle out loud, not beat by beat but line by line—for the meaning of it, and not for the patterns. "'By the stream the fox and she-fox stood,'" she read, "'Nose to nose beneath the stars / Dancing the music of the woods.'

"That's so lovely, Elisa," she interrupted herself, looked up. "It really is. Then something happens in this woodsy paradise, something devastating. Listen: 'Then from the north a fierce wind blew / And broke the starry dance apart / By the stream where the fox and she-fox stood.' And now the final quatrain: 'The stars blinked out, also the moon. / The air went silent, cold, and hard / By the stream where the fox and the she-fox stood / Dancing the music of the woods.'"

"The meter's off," I said.

"But it's very close, Elisa. And the meaning is there. The question is, What's happened since then? You've had a precipitous slide toward the mediocre."

I must have looked at her strangely.

"Precipitous," she said. "That's a word for your Book of Words. Which, by the way, I hope you're maintaining."

"Doing my best, Dr. Charmin," I said.

"You're not going to tell me what's wrong, are you?"

I shook my head. You could hear the hand of the clock ticking the afternoon off. "It's just that I keep messing up," I finally said. "And I don't know how to fix things. And I don't know where I belong."

"Ah," she said, after a moment. "The human condition."

I nodded. "I guess."

"You wrote 'Fox-Trot' for someone, didn't you, Elisa?"

I nodded again, but only vaguely.

"Did you show it to that person?"

I shook my head no.

"Maybe you should, Elisa. Sometimes that's what poems are for." The loosened hair had laid a new fringe across Dr. Charmin's face. She smoothed it back with her hand.

14

THE NEXT DAY was the thirteenth, a
Friday. The sun had come down hard the
afternoon before and melted things, but at dusk the
temperature had dropped, so now, outside, it was a
stalactite world, heavy icicles daggering down from the
gutter lines and window ledges. On the walk to school
Jilly said that she couldn't wait for summer, when all
the dirty snow would be gone and all the flowers burst
open with blooms. She said she had been building up
a garden in her mind like some garden she had seen on
one of her shows—dahlias, gladiolas, lilies, but not the
orange lilies that were, she said, far too common. She

would plant the garden along the back edge of the yard and bring Mom one fresh blooming stalk each day. "That's all I can think of, Elisa," she said. "If Dad doesn't make it home, I mean."

In her blue beret, tan leather gloves, and long woolen coat, Jilly looked, just then, like a snow queen. We walked along not saying much, and there was a sort of peace to that.

At the doors to the school, past Romance Hill, we went our separate ways. That morning, as usual, there was a crowd—flying hollers and high fives I had to dodge my way around until I'd made it down toward the end of my hall, within seeing distance of my locker. I thought I saw Theo standing there, and then I realized I had—that he'd been there, seen me, taken off. He had a special way of vanishing, Theo. He'd thin-aired himself once again.

"Theo," I almost called after him. "Theo!" But what would be the use? There'd be no turning him around. I grabbed my locker lock and dialed in: Thirty-six. Nineteen. Two. I pulled the lock; it clicked. I swung open the door, hung my coat on the hook, bent down, and I had to dig around a bit at first, but then, absolutely, I saw it—the sheet of paper, folded to a square.

THE BORDER ROAD SKATING
& HUMANE SOCIETY
IS PLEASED TO ANNOUNCE

The John Mischa Petkovich First Annual
Interpretive Free Skate Competition
February 28, 4 PM
Open to the Public
Registration Required

Here are some words for your Book of Words, if you ever decide you need one:

Recrudescence, which is to be revived.

Forgiveness, which is the place that every story turns, the chance we give each other.

Dear Dad,

I've been writing poems and making a Book of Words.

I've taught myself ice-skating.

I had a friend and then something happened.

Mom's been really sad.

Jilly's been nice.

But.

I'm not tracking the changes for you anymore. You have to see them for yourself.

Fifteen days.

Four o'clock.

The Border Road Rink.

Please.

Get back to me.

> *Love,*
> *Elisa*

15

THAT NIGHT Mom joined us downstairs for dinner. We had canned soup and the kind of cheese that's separated by plastic squares, a couple of old crackers. Jilly lit two candles and put them on plates in the table's center, then turned the lights down low. All through dinner, she caught Mom up on all the soaps, and when she got things wrong, I said so. "You're such a pain in the butt, Elisa," Jilly said, and I said the least she could do was keep the soaps straight, because it felt good, for once, to be jerks with each other, it felt right and normal.

After dinner Mom said she could use a good dessert, and so I stood and opened up the freezer—

dug in through the bags of frozen peas and sausages, the boxes of French toast, the slab of steak that had bruised to blue, the cans of concentrate. All I could find were three cups of overfrosted cherry ice, and that's what we ate, with those little wooden spoons, scraping out the sweet like it was the most important job in the entire world. Jilly's lips turned the color of the ice, which upped her glamour quotient. Mom pointed to a place on the left side of her forehead that had gotten what she called a sudden cold.

The wicks burned deep into the wax and gave us shadow faces, and I thought about the pond under the moon at night and all I'd learned to see in the dark, all I'd learned to look for. I thought of all that would change once I told my secret, but the time, in fact, had come. "Mom?" I said, for we were all still sitting there. "I'm going to need your help. I need a dress, but a dress that I can skate in. I need you to make me pretty for one day."

Mom looked at me, then looked at Jilly, then looked at me again, and what I want noted right here, for the permanent record, is that Jilly will grow up to be my mom. She will look the same way lit up by old candlelight, the same way taken by surprise, the same way not believing and then perhaps believing, the same big eyes and the same O!-question-mark lips.

"You want what?" Jilly said.

"Did you say a dress?" my mother asked.

"A dress," I said, "for skating." And then, as the candles burned low in their wax, I told my sister and my mother of my own private history—which is a story, the way I told it, of expeditions and stolen skates, of paths through woods, of snow. Of a forgotten trail to a forgotten pond, of a sunken marble girl. I told them that I'd found music up inside my bones, that speed is powered by your knees, that it doesn't matter who you are—your arms can make you lovely.

But I didn't tell them about loving Theo. I didn't say I'd written to Dad. That's what undercover operatives do. They pick and choose their truths.

THERE WERE ONLY fifteen days between our soup and cheese dinner and the John Mischa Petkovich Interpretive Free Skate competition. Mom and Jilly went to work at once, that very night—studying their fashion magazines for color concepts, yanking dresses out of their closets to test out shoulder styles and decorative bits and all the things I will formally confess right here that I have never noticed. Every now and then they would make me stand up and turn, first slowly, then more quickly, so that they could configure, in their own minds' eyes, an image of me as a skater. We did the work in that part of the house that wasn't a room or a hallway—their dresses and magazines in a messy stew. Jilly sat on the steps with a notebook on her knees while Mom contemplated hem lengths and leotards, sleeves that flared and didn't, the kinds of beads you could see from a distance, even if the spotlights weren't on.

Saturday, the next day, we set off for the rink—just Mom and me—so I could get, as my mother put it, a mental map. We had to drive straight past the school and Romance Hill, which still had the aftermath of Valentine's hearts lying about, toward the two cross streets that make for the minuscule heartbeat of our town—one street with the shops, one street with the institutions: the library, the post office, the old opera house that had stood empty for years until someone turned it into a movie theater.

Border Road Rink was beyond all that, on the industrial road where civilization ends. You might have thought the rink had been built whole centuries ago, but Dad once said that though it wasn't quite that old, you could trace its beginnings back to a few heroic guys who pulled skaters out of thawing ponds. A glass case inside boasted the antique stuff—the rescue hooks, the double-runner skates, the old rabbit-fur mufflers that the skating ladies wore.

From the outside the rink looked like a concrete eyeball that had fallen to the asphalt from the sky. An old faded blue sign announced the public-skate hours, and the door was one of those heavy metal doors you imagine needing only for maximum-security prisons. Even when it was cold outside, it was always colder in the rink, where there was no direct sun, only the frosted-over glass of windows that ran high along three sides. The light that came from those windows was the color of smog. It told you nothing about the weather outside.

Running along the two long sides were two sets of wooden bleachers, and at the far short end there was the little cave where they stowed the old Zamboni, a monster that lived like the last of its kind. On the other short end, nearest the door and ticket booth, was the coffee shop where the artifacts were housed and where you could buy hot choco-late, coffee, or candy bars—anything and all things for three dollars.

Above the coffee shop was a balcony that you reached by a set of wooden stairs, and on that day there were little girls up there in leotards draping themselves across a ballet barre. A tiny old woman with tight, wound-up hair was standing before them counting out first position, second position, fifth. She had a scarf the size of a quilt around her neck and a you-will-listen voice, and all the girls did that finger-pointing thing, with their arms just as high as they could reach them.

Still, it was the ice itself that had me in awe. I hadn't understood how purely white and smooth rink ice could be, how perfectly even end to end, without twigs or wings or bug eyes.

My pond was smaller than that rink, and the rink was slippery smooth, and that day it had been divided into long halves by six orange cones, one half for beginners in a big group lesson, one half for one girl in pink and her exceedingly French-looking coach. He stood on the ice in a pair of fuzzy boots, demonstrating the attitudes he wanted. Then he stood back and stroked his almost-white mustache while the pinked girl did her best to imitate him. There were times when even I could tell that the girl had it all wrong, and when that happened, her coach walked straight out to her, grabbed her limbs, and pushed them into proper place. He worked her like she was sculpture. Then she'd try the move again, and it would be right or it would be wrong, and he'd nod or shake, as moved to do. "She's pretty, isn't she?" my mother said, and of course she was, how couldn't she be—so pinked like that, so small.

Mom had said that I should have my own pair of skates for the coming competition, that her old, stolen, nicked-up skates would not do, and so we headed off toward the skate shop, down the alley between a pair of those bleachers. "My daughter's skating in the Petkovich competition," my mother told the little Geppetto man. She leaned across the counter and gave him one of her most irresistible Hollywood smiles.

"Well then," he said.

"Size eight, I think."

"The options are many." Giving my mom a wink, Geppetto pointed to the benches, where I went to sit while he went into a dark back room to sort through boxes. All the time we waited, my mother studied the photographs of skaters that were posted on the corkboard walls of the shop. "Oh," she said, "I always wanted to be a skater. Look at how pretty they all are." She got up close to one particular photograph and with deep appreciation squinted. When at last Geppetto reappeared, he plopped himself down on a rolling stool.

I tried skate after skate over sock after sock. In the end he sold us the most premium skates that came with the blades already on, because we didn't have time, as my mother said, to wait for screws. "Leotards?" she asked him, and good thing he sold those, too. My mother gave him her credit card. He boxed things up. We were done.

It was on the way out of the rink that I saw the stack of flyers that announced the competition; they'd been put out on the ledge near the ticket booth. Immediately then I understood: Theo had taken Lila skating, but he'd also thought of me.

"Looks like the public-skate session is about to start," my mother said, of the crowds that had begun to work their way through.

"We should go," I said.

"It's so exciting," she said, and she smiled in a way she hadn't smiled in weeks, in a way that made me wonder inside if things were getting fixed with Dad.

Mom would spend the rest of the day out, at the crafts and fabric store. She'd go through bolts and bolts and bolts, she'd later say, testing each fabric for its shimmer and glow, keeping my auburn hair in mind. She'd buy a new pair of shears, packs of needles in every sharp size. Then later that day she'd climb the thin steps up to the attic and carry her old Singer downstairs. She'd fit it on the kitchen table, like a fancy centerpiece.

ONCE DAD AND I went treasuring when I was nine years old. It was summer, already hot at only daybreak, and you could feel the water in the air. "Grab your bucket, Sweetie," Dad had said, and at dawn we had set out, him holding my hand because I wanted him to, because I put mine right in his.

That was back when our neighborhood was still mostly trees and such old houses that, one by one, they'd all come down. Where Mrs. Garland's house would soon be there was a very giant hole and, inside that hole, some old foundations. Dad said that one day I'd learn about Pompeii and see the resemblance, but for right then, he said, we should take a look around and see what we might see. "History," Dad had said, "at our very fingertips." And "Be careful where you step, Elisa. History takes courage."

I found fragments of flowerpots and the slats of an old wood fence, the cloudy glass of a broken jar. I found a single die that I slipped into my bucket, and an old red metal fire truck, very miniature and rusted. I saved that, too. At the bottom of a pile of chipped bricks I found a dress that must have once belonged to a baby doll. I found an empty canister for film. I found a bit of Christmas foil. I found a wooden hanger.

The sun kept climbing up its ladder. My neck got trickled wet. "Elisa." I remember the excitement in Dad's voice. "Sweetheart, come here and see." And of course I ran, because my dad was my dad and the very best in all the world at treasure hunts. I remember the sloshing-around-of-metal sound that came from my peach-colored bucket. I remember standing in the shade of his long shadow. "Do you know what that is?" he asked, reaching a coin, silver and round, toward me.

"Money?" I'd said.

"Time," he said. "A nineteen twenty-two silver dollar."

"Oh" is all I knew to say.

I lifted the coin out of Dad's hand and held it as appreciatively as I could. He turned it over, showed me the serious face of Liberty, the way something looking like sun rays shot right up through her hair. He turned it again and showed me the eagle, looking confident as any bird on any silver day.

"I bequeath it unto you, Princess of Dawn," he said. "In honor of your courage."

Princess, I remember he said. And I remember courage.

A FTER CHRISTIAN DIES on the battle-
field, Roxane retires to a nunnery to mourn
the man she thinks she loved. Cyrano, for her sake,
maintains the charade—visiting Roxane to lift her
spirits, suffering injustices he won't speak of, assur-
ing the woman he loves that she is right to go on
loving the memory of another. Cyrano has grown
poor. His coat is wearing thin. His words are making another playwright famous. But what does he
do, for fourteen years? He attends to Roxane's fantasy. "It was written / that I should build for others
and be forgotten . . ." he says. "I stand below in

dark—'tis all my story— / while others climb to snatch the kiss of glory."

Here's what I think, when I think about it more: Beauty is a cruel deception, true. But the greatest tragedy of all is letting invisibility win. It's choosing to give up the thing you want because you think you don't deserve it.

I got to school extremely early the next morning. Most of the classrooms were still dark behind their doors, and the janitor was whistling a tune from years ago. The sun through the front windows was hitting the lockers just so, forcing a little spray of gleam, and from beneath the door of the teachers' lounge came the high-in-the-nose stink of coffee. Down the hall, just near the auditorium, was Theo's locker. I'd seen him there a million times before, holding court with Lila, and I'd seen him there in the early morning, before her bus rolled in. I was taking my chances, I understood that. I had brought my 1922 with me, for courage more than luck, and I'd clipped up my hair, and I wore my best jeans, and I roamed that hallway, waiting—running my hand across the silver beaks of all those lockers, giving each a touch. Up the one side of that hall of lockers, down the other, until finally I saw him.

He'd come in through a side door with his hood lifted like a monk's. There was some old snow crud in the wedges of his boots that made them go *pa-phaaaa, pa-phaaaa* as he walked. It wasn't like we were the only two about; already the empty spaces between things were filling up with elbows, backpacks. Over by the corner where Theo had come in, Mr. Sue and Mrs. Sue were in the midst of some long talk, and suddenly Mr. Marcoroon was there, holding tea in a Styrofoam cup. When Theo saw me, he tucked his chin toward his chest. He headed for his locker, dialed in, opened the thing with a crack.

"Hey," I said, for I'd followed him.

"Hey," he said. He swung the locker door open to where I was. I circled behind him, to the other side. I waited for an apology. An explanation. Nothing.

"You know this is ridiculous," I said, "don't you? There's no reason why we can't be friends."

"Just doing my part to keep the peace," Theo said.

"Yeah, well," I said. "But I miss you." My mouth was wads-of-cotton dry. I fished for the coin in my pocket.

He pulled his head out of his locker and looked up at me. His eyes seemed bruised and contradicted. "You should leave it alone, Elisa," he finally said, standing and slamming the locker door.

"Isn't it just a little bit bizarre—being afraid of the person you love?" Maybe I was desperate and therefore desperate sounding, but he had started walking down the hall. Away from me and into the crowd. Away and farther away from us. We split and came together, like a river over rocks. I grabbed his arm and held it, wouldn't let go. I didn't care if Margie slunk by. Or if Bolten saw. Or Lila.

Mr. Marcoroon was back and headed our way, and suddenly there was Dr. Charmin, pale as a snow-drop flower in a royal purple suit, some of her hair already loose from the knot she wore. Her eyes traveled down to my hand on Theo's arm. She stopped, I shook my head, she walked on past.

"You don't get it, do you?" Theo said at last, pulling us both toward the lockered wall, out of the way of things.

"Get what?" I freed his arm, turned to face him.

"That I'm not afraid for me. I'm afraid for you. You don't know what she's capable of." He looked so deep into my eyes that I felt my stomach turn, my heart go wild and helpless.

"What can she do to me, Theo?" I said. "Honestly?"

"You have no idea," he said. "I'm just trying to keep you safe."

"I'm skating in that competition," I said. "The one you left me the flyer on."

"Yeah?" He smiled faintly. "You better win."

"Will you come to watch?" I almost pleaded with him.

"Are you kidding? That would start a war."

"Is it really going to be like this?"

"At least for now."

"But do you love her?"

"I'm *caught up* with her," he said, "and there's a difference."

"You could choose, you know, not to be." And I was about to say more. About to retrace the sad history of Roxane and Cyrano. About to say that tragedy is not inevitable, that it works far better in old books than in real life, but then I saw her—saw Lila—fuming down the hall with all her ardent anger. She had the snap-snap walk of a model on a runway, and her jacket was open so that it winged away from her, making her seem like some prehistoric bird. Anyone near her dodged her. The corridor went wide empty before her, the crowd scuttled off to either side.

"Didn't I tell you, Cantor," she said when she

reached the two of us at the lockered wall, "to leave Theo alone?"

"Isn't this," I asked, "a free country?"

"Give it up. You're a charity case. You're not in his league and you never will be." She pressed a hand to my left shoulder and put her mouth up near my ear: "You're going to pay for this, Elisa. You wait."

"Lila," Theo said, in a placating voice. "We were just—"

"Don't you dare say it's Honors English again. I'm not that stupid, you know."

"—talking," Theo said. "We were just talking."

"There's no 'just' here, Theo. This is crazy." She looked as if she were about to blow. Her hand pressed harder against my shoulder. A little crowd had formed, but at some distance. I didn't know, I really didn't, what would happen next.

And then I heard a familiar voice; I saw a familiar royal purple. "Everything okay here, I presume? You're all now headed off to classes?" She stood there for a moment, Dr. Charmin did, eyeing us, with her arms crossed against her chest.

"Yes, Dr. Charmin," Theo said.

"Yes," I said. And: "Thank you."

After school that day I went straight to Dr. Charmin's classroom. She was there, at her chalkboard, ghosting the day into the past, and she'd removed her suit jacket and set it aside, let her hair all the way out of its knot. I could almost see her then as she must have been when she first began her Book of Words. When there were still a million poems, stories, plays that she hadn't yet learned to decipher.

"Dr. Charmin," I said.

"Yes?" she turned, and whatever thought she'd been having had by now been replaced by another. She seemed pleased to see me, relieved almost, as if I'd had a choice to make and finally made the right one. "What can I do for you, Miss Cantor?"

I didn't actually know. I couldn't tell her why I'd

come. Maybe it's easier, not being invisible alone. Maybe it's better to find an ally. I walked to the first row of seats, unharnessed my backpack, sunk down into a chair. Dr. Charmin leaned against her desk, facing me. "I've been thinking," I finally said, "about Cyrano."

"He's hard to forget," she said, "once you know him." There was a little puff of dust on her cheek. A tired crease above her eyes, kindness in them.

"I was thinking about his last monologue. That line he says: 'It is the hope forlorn that seals the poet.'"

"Ah." Dr. Charmin looked past me then, to the windows beyond. "Well. Many things seal a poet. Courage, for example. And a particular way of seeing."

"Maybe," I said.

"No," she said, looking directly at me now. "That's true. Poems are there to be discovered. And poets stand right there, behind them."

"What does Cyrano have in the end?" I asked.

"His panache," she said after a moment. "His dignity. The love of his beloved."

"But he's dying," I said, "and he still has that stupid nose. And what good is Roxane watering his grave with tears going to do?"

"Well, that's why you were right, Elisa. It is a tragedy." She gave that word a little sun. She shrugged her shoulders slyly.

"You know what I hate?" I declared, feeling emboldened.

"What's that?"

"The rules of love."

"Rotten." She smiled. "Through and through. But if they weren't so rotten, what would poets do?"

"Hope less forlornly, I guess."

"Yes. Maybe they would. But oh, how the poems themselves would suffer."

She looked at me and something caught in her throat. The lines above her forehead crossed, and all of a sudden, she was laughing. Just the smallest oddest ripple of a laugh, a rueful laugh that, it seemed to me, mixed the present with the past. The thinnest tear ran down her cheek, a minor stream of mascara.

"You know what I love?" Dr. Charmin said after she'd caught her breath.

"Tragedies," I said, "and teaching them."

"True," she smiled. "But there are other things. Like a poem called 'Wild Geese' by Mary Oliver. I have a copy," she said, "that I've been meaning to give to you. To have for when you need it." She turned and rifled through some papers on her desk. She handed me a Xerox copy. "For you," she said.

I leaned across the space between us and took the paper from her hands. "Courage," she said, "is all. Remember that."

Wild Geese

You do not have to be good.
You do not have to walk on your knees
for a hundred miles through the desert, repenting.
You only have to let the soft animal of your body
  love what it loves.
Tell me about despair, yours, and I will tell you mine.
Meanwhile the world goes on.
Meanwhile the sun and the clear pebbles of the rain
are moving across the landscapes,
over the prairies and the deep trees,
the mountains and the rivers.
Meanwhile the wild geese, high in the clean blue air,
are heading home again.
Whoever you are, no matter how lonely,
the world offers itself to your imagination,
calls to you like the wild geese, harsh and exciting—
over and over announcing your place
in the family of things.

ALL THROUGH the next several days I kept the poem with me—in the front pocket of my pants, on my nightstand, tucked inside a sock. I left Theo and Lila in their tangle. I steered clear, for all our sakes. I wouldn't look up when Lila steamed at me, refused to give her the slightest chance to make good on her threats.

I focused, instead, on the skating. Went out to the pond with my new pair of skates and slowly broke them in, bending the creases into the ankles just so, sitting right on top of the blades. I could go so much deeper on my edges because of this, and also I could carry more speed, get greater height on my toe-pick jumps, hold the landings longer. I took whole songs to the pond in my head and choreographed my way straight through them, because that, of course, is what an interpretive free skate competition is: They play the music. You interpret. Mom had called and they'd read her the rules, and this is what she told me: That we competitors would hear a chosen clip of music three times on the rink, then be escorted back to the dressing rooms, which were supposedly soundproof. Then, one by one, they'd call our names and we'd be returned to the rink and asked to skate to the music as if we'd always known the music, to its stresses and accents, to its story, though Mom didn't say the last part, of course. It was just something that I knew from loving poems, from the things that Dr. Charmin taught me. Out on the pond I was skating to remembered songs, riding the crest of violins.

At home Mom had settled on spearmint green. Long sleeves, she'd decided, and a scooped-out

20

THAT SATURDAY I rose before dawn, when the stars were still out and the moon had traveled to the far end of the yard. I reread Dad's letter and I reread Mary Oliver's poem, then I tucked both inside my Stash O' Nature box for when I would need them again. Courage is the step you take after the step just taken. That was something else that I was learning.

The night before, Mom and Jilly had hung my competition dress on a wooden hanger and hooked that hanger over my bedroom door; the dress shone like a second sweep of stars. Every seam of that dress was tight, every pearl sewn into its shell of sequin. Mom had found my color at last, and my color, just for the extremely permanent record, is spearmint green.

It had been decided that I'd wear a pair of spandex pants to the rink, a purple turtleneck, tights, one of Jilly's white sweaters. That my hair would be straightened, then curled, that I'd wear three coats of mascara, that we'd go with a ruddy color for my cheeks and a reddish brown for my lips, that we'd do all the primping in my room. Talk about tedious. You need a talent for sitting if you want any shot at beauty, a high tolerance for mirror glare. And then you need to fit your real face into the face you've been drawn into, which is an art in itself.

"You've got to stop twitching," Jilly said.

"You've got to be kidding," I said back.

"You're a girl," Jilly said. "Get used to it."

"There are all kinds of girls."

"Will you stop?" my mother called from down the hall. "You're giving me a headache. Both of you." I thought about Mom, and all she did not know was coming. I imagined her with her tubes and her brushes before her mirrored glass, orchestrating her own metamorphosis. I smiled a little covert smile as Jilly glossed my lips. She sighed and rolled her lovely eyes.

"You are the worst beauty client," Jilly said, reaching for a Kleenex to dab away a smudge. "Ever."

I shrugged.

"I'm doing my best here," she said.

"You're a pro."

I sat quietly while she finished the job. Put my mind on the ice and the edges of my skates, set my conjured skates to song. Thought of all the different ways the coming competition might go, of how it might feel to skate before a crowd. I did not hear the doorbell when it rang. I did not hear (though Jilly told me later) when it rang again. Maybe vaguely I heard Mom say, "All right, you two. I'll get it." Maybe vaguely heard her open her door. Did hear her heading down the stairs.

"You expecting someone, Jilly?" I said, finally snapping out of my daze.

"Nnnhnnmm." She had the hair clip in her mouth, the finishing touch.

"No one at all?"

"Nnnnhmm."

Suddenly, acutely aware of all things, I leaned toward my door and listened to the goings-on downstairs. It couldn't be Dad, I thought. It couldn't be; that wasn't our plan. And if it wasn't Dad and wasn't one of Jilly's billion friends, who had come to visit? I heard my mother's high voice and a lower, shy voice. I heard a mumble and a laugh. "Jilly, will you excuse me for a moment?" I said. I opened the door and unceremoniously flew.

My mother swiveled as I rumbled down the stairs. "I was just about to go and get you," she said. She had a sly, sweet smile on her perfectly tinted face. She had a glimmer in her eyes, small reflected parts of Theo.

I stared past my mom, toward him. "But what are

you doing here?" I asked. I touched my fingers to my face, felt every inch of spandexed, turtlenecked skin go red. I looked up the staircase, saw Jilly smiling. I turned the other way, and there was Mom. I turned and there was Theo again, no ring in his ear, no spikes in his hair, no fear in his eyes. Just Theo.

"Choosing," Theo said. "To come. To wish you luck, in person, on the big day."

"You're choosing," I said. I hoped my smile was where Jilly had drawn it. I hoped my eyes looked like mine.

"Yes." He smiled.

"Good choice," I said.

"Yeah," he said. "I thought so." I wanted to laugh. I wanted to dance. I wanted to grab that guy and kiss him.

"Were you planning on introductions, Elisa?" Mom asked.

"But you've already met." I felt my face go red again.

"He hasn't met me," said Jilly, who had made

her way down the stairs.

"This is Theo," I said, giving Jilly the don't-you-dare-ruin-this stare. "And this"—I bowed faux fawningly—"is Jilly. My personal beautician."

"And sister."

"Excellent work." Theo nodded.

"Can you stay awhile, Theo?" Mom interjected. "We have chips, I think. And salsa."

"If we're lucky," Jilly said, and laughed, then stopped after she caught Mom's eye.

"I can't," Theo said. "At least I can't today."

"Okay," I said. "Yeah."

"Skate your heart out, Elisa."

"I will."

"Don't get a swelled head if you win."

"Yeah. Right."

"Call me later, if you want to."

THE PARKING LOT at the Border Road Rink was thick with cars and people, and by the time we finally got there, I was overcome with nerves. Theo coming had been the best thing ever, but it was complicated, too, for suddenly I had so much more to skate for and something new, perhaps, to lose.

"Will you look at this?" Jilly said as we pulled up, in her I'm-impressed voice. And right like that her hand went up, like she was the homecoming queen. It's belief defying, the quantities of people Jilly knows, the way anywhere you go, it is her party.

"I don't think I can do this," I said, and Mom said, "Of course you can." But she was still somewhat giddy over the early afternoon, and what did she know about ice-skating, really, and what could I tell her just then about the surprise I had planned for us all and how I was suddenly overcome with nerves? I'd been practicing on a pond at night, teaching myself my own tricks. I'd been channeling music the way I hear music, without the benefit— not once—of a critique. Theo had come, and Dad had promised, but isn't the future always unknown, isn't it, still, out of reach? Panache, I thought, and I held my head high—across the parking lot, through the door, in through the wintry blast of the Border Road Rink, toward whatever waited.

The little girls were competing first in their sherbet-colored dresses. They were out on the ice with their sweaters on, warming up crossovers and waltz jumps. Muzak floated from the speakers above. The crowd was far from settled. Across the way, right down below the bleachers, a narrow table had been dressed with a thick white cloth, and behind it were six chairs, each enthroned before the rink. Two of the judges had taken their places and were watching the sherbet girls through spectacles. I scanned the bleachers and the milling crowd. *Elisa,* Dad had written, *I will be there. Skate your heart out,* Theo had said. And I'd said, *I will.*

"You better hurry up and change," Jilly said, but there was plenty of time before my age group came on, and I knew from watching my mother for years that you should never let your dress get old. I would reveal it when I revealed myself on the ice at the John Mischa Petkovich First Annual Interpretive Free Skate competition. I would take my chances then.

You had to go through the coffee shop, past the case of history, to get to the ladies' changing room. I went that way, with all my things—my dress, Jilly's sweater, my skates, the little competitor's name badge that had come in the mail after Mom had sent in her registration check. I went that way with my head held high. *Courage is all, Elisa.*

The changing-room door was one of those swing-open doors that led to yet another door, that opened on an angle to the room. There were lockers on either side, and one square window in one corner, letting in milky-colored light. The bathrooms were at a right angle to this room, a couple of stalls behind another swinging door, and a number of the older contestants had already gathered, their dresses hung from a cord that diagonaled across the ceiling and had hung from it, on one end, a pair of drying tights. I hung my dress up with the rest of them and looped the badge around its neck. I tied my skates together and hung them from my shoulder, and went out again, through the two doors, through the coffee shop.

The sherbet girls were getting the judges' instructions now. They were clustered in one corner, waiting for their music to begin, and Mom and Jilly were already seated somewhere in the stands. I went up the stairs to the balcony to watch. To practice putting music in my bones. To be alone before my moment. I breathed out and in, long breaths. I telegraphed the calm of the marble girl, tried to conjure Theo laughing on the ice, at night.

Dad, I thought, shouldn't you be here by now?

But when I scanned the crowd, I couldn't find him.

I waited a really long time. I waited, pushing all my thoughts around and around in my head. I waited and I hoped, and I waited and I dared. I waited and I watched the others skating. Five sherbet girls had already performed in the free skate. A sunshiny song played on the P.A. system. I'd scanned the crowd again and not found Dad, and that's when I got hit with the bad feeling. It was like a hand reaching up into my gut and yanking it all around. I stood, because it hurt to sit. I left my chair, walked across the balcony, crept down the narrow stairs. I stepped toward the coffee shop, the skates on my shoulder toeing each other.

It was when I was turning the corner by the coffee shop that I saw them—Lila and her friends. Lila's hair was tied up in a bun, with the bangs across her face, and she was laughing. You don't think pretty girls can ever be ugly, but make no mistake: Cruelty is its own brand of hideous. Lila had a secret of her own, and I knew as well as I knew anything that it had taken action against me.

The dressing-room door was swinging shut behind them; they were all four wild with power. It took them a moment before they saw me, and when they did, they all raised their hands and pointed. As if I were an exotic animal found out in the woods. As if I weren't a girl, too, just like them. They stumbled on their tall high-heeled boots, laughing. They cupped their hands over their high-gloss mouths, snorted through their perky noses.

"Did you think I was kidding, Elisa?" Lila said, coming close, tossing her bangs back with a gloved hand. "Did you think I didn't mean it when I said you'd asked for trouble?"

"I don't really think about you, Lila," I said, "to be honest." A face-saving lie, best I could do.

"You think about me all the time," she said, "wishing you had what I have, but you don't and won't and never will."

She wanted to prolong the fight. I didn't. She wanted some confession. I wouldn't fall. She wanted me to pledge against any future friendship with Theo. Impossible. I knew another kind of damage had been done, an irreversible something, and I knew that there'd be little time to make it right. I knew before I swung open the one dressing-room door and pulled at the other. I knew before I saw anything at all—before I reached for my dress on the diagonal clothesline, before I looked about that room and saw Jilly's sweater tossed into one corner, my name badge tossed into another. The cork floor of the dressing room told the truth in haiku—every pearl of my dress, every sequin, fallen like snow, so many bits of spearmint-colored thread like hair after a cutting.

There was no one there—no one and nothing but me and the milky-colored light and the sunshine song I could still partway hear, even though the room was supposed to be soundproof. I took the dress from the line and held it in my hands, touched all the places where the pearls had been, the burst, ruined fabric. There wasn't a single sequin left.

There were thirty minutes before my warm-up session was set to begin. Thirty minutes. On that bench, in that room with the wrong-colored light, I buried my face in my hands. My mascara was a river, then, black as the deepest sorrow.

22

YOU EVER HAVE IT HAPPEN that a power so infinitely bigger than you becomes you, for just a fraction of a while? You ever dig in past your list of words and live something you will never rightly know the language for? I knew the other girls in my competition class would be showing up soon, and I knew nothing would be gained from any more crying. I had two choices, and those choices were these: Skate in the spandex or hide the ruin of the dress in Jilly's sweater. I chose to wear the dress, of course. It had been made for me with loving care.

My face was trails of black and transplanted lip

gloss. I scrubbed it clean. Only my hair clips had held, and the smooth, Jilly-quality straightness of my curled hair, which I was extra careful with as I slipped off my turtleneck and stepped into the spearmint dress. I zipped. I heard the sound of someone coming and threw the sweater on, buttoned it up, bottom to top, as quickly as I could. I swept the pearls and sequins from the floor with my hand, retrieved my name badge, put it on. Sat on the bench and laced up my skates. Tested their tightness. Laced meticulously again. It was what my family would have wanted me to do. It was what Theo expected.

All through this the other skaters had come in, unhooking their dresses from the line, zippering themselves into their swatches of pink, their gauze-for-skirts, their yellow-and-black checkerboards, their sparkles. They were girls-who-knew-one-another girls—girls I might have seen around, but none of whom I was friends with—and at the one end of the room, where a skinny mirror was, they gathered, checking their panty lines and rouging their faces. That they were Border Road Rink members was clear, and that I wasn't one of them was even clearer, as sometimes their talk would throttle down to a hush and one would look at me, and the others would follow, and then they all would shake their heads and shrug their shoulders. There was a big, old-fashioned clock in the room, and the minutes went by slowly. I sat where I sat until the sherbet girls were done and some official someone in a navy-blue parka swung open the second dressing-room door and said, "Your turn, girls. Time for warm-up."

I was the last of the competitors through the dressing-room doors, through the old coffee shop, past the case of history. The last to step into the iced rink air, into the noise of all those people on the bleachers who turned the names of the Border Road girls into some kind of pandemonium. I knew Mom and Jilly were there, and Lila somewhere with her crowd, but I didn't know a thing about Dad. I was the last to take the ice that day, and it was smooth and white as vanilla ice cream.

After warm-up the judges called us over and reviewed the rules. I kept my eyes on the ice, stood outside the members' circle. When the lead judge pulled our names out of a hat and gave us the skating order, I didn't complain that I was to go first. When they played the music we were to interpret that night, I let it spigot through my bones.

Then the others left the rink.

Then it was me and everything that I am made of.

Once when I was a younger, I saw Mom and Dad dancing in that place in the house that isn't a room and isn't a hallway. It was late at night, and being thirsty, I'd gotten up to fill my cup with water. They never saw me sitting there, on the top of the steps, looking down, while the moon through the windows lit their way. I never told. Dad was making the music up, humming it softly over Mom's slender shoulder, and Mom was counting slow-slow-quick-quick, slow-slow-quick-quick, quiet as a whisper. She was wearing a nightdress that looked like a gown, and her hair was loose on her shoulders. Dad was wearing his pajama trousers and a brand-new, crisp T-shirt. They moved like ice was at their feet and music in their bones, and I sat there wishing that I could dance like them, that I would someday hold a moment.

I can't tell you the name of the music that I skated to that night. I can tell you that it began with four quick strokes across the ice, then a long, deep swoop toward the right, hands touching hands overhead to make an oval, and next a turn. Then I was skating backward, crossover after crossover, readying myself, readying everyone who was watching, for a high-as-the-moon waltz jump. I timed the jump to land on the cusp of a crescendo, and then I held that edge fastidiously. And then the music changed and razzled up its tempo, and I took three quick steps into a split jump, which is, I meant to mention, my brand-new move. Just a scissors split, but it cut the music fine, sent me up above the barrier, then set me down again, because something was happening inside that song, the violins were lamenting, and it was this lament that carried me down the rink on one long spiral. Despite Lila. Despite the member girls. Despite the pearls that I had swept off the floor. I couldn't hear anything but the music. I didn't know if the crowd was with me. All I knew was that I was holding my own kind of moment, that I was making and roaring, and that this was the Cantor legacy. I can't tell you the name of the music that I skated to that night, but I can say that I was safe inside it, that I was nothing but song until it stopped.

It was only after I was done that I heard my name called out three ways—my mother's voice, my sister's voice, my dad's. Two voices from the bleachers, Dad's from near the entrance, beyond the ticket booth, where, I know now, he'd been standing all along, keeping his own counsel while I skated, for he had come home. I heard their voices in the clear, bright air, and I heard my name, called over and over, announcing my place in the wild, good family of things.

ACKNOWLEDGMENTS

Every book has a beginning, and *Undercover* began on a rainy day in conversation with the marvelous publisher Laura Geringer. She had been asking questions about the journey that has been my life and the things I've loved, and she was listening. Within days the story was writing itself. It had, by Laura, been found.

Along the way, the book benefited enormously from the kindness, steadfastness, and intelligence of Senior Editor Jill Santopolo, and from the care and ingenuity of Assistant Editor Lindsey Alexander. It was given a most glorious cover by Chad W.

Beckerman, who was assisted by Associate Creative Director Martha Rago. Almost every mistake I was inclined to make was eradicated by the fabulously precise copyeditor Renée Cafiero; if mistakes remain, they are mine, for sure. My wonderful film agent, Sean Daily, has read this book with care and made significant contributions to it. My longtime, one-and-only literary agent, Amy Rennert, cheered me through every draft of this, our first novel, with her always-present optimism and smarts. My son, Jeremy, let me read him critical pages so that I could benefit from the wisdom he has always so generously granted. My husband, Bill, gave me room to work and think.

The night I learned that *Undercover* had been bought by HarperCollins, I raced to my parents' house to tell them the news that a lifetime dream, the publishing of a novel, was about to be realized. My mother sat in her chair at her table, reached for my hand, and said, "Beth, your time has come." Sadly, my mother did not live to see this book come fully to life, but where there is goodness on these pages, it is hers.

This is a book of fiction, ultimately. The story was imagined, the characters conjured. Not one member of the Cantor family is to be construed as representative of any member of my own. But I did once, long ago, teach myself Elisa's basic skating moves on a pond in Boston, and later I wore the very dress I describe here in a skating competition. And once I had an English teacher named Dr. Dewsnap who believed in me, even when my poems didn't work and my voice faltered in classroom readings.